Andy Whitbeck

UNCLE WIGGILY'S STORY BOOK

BY HOWARD R. GARIS

Platt & Munk, Publishers • New York
A division of Grosset & Dunlap

Copyright 1921, 1949 by Platt & Munk, Publishers.
Cover illustration copyright © 1987 by Daniel San Souci.
All rights reserved.
Published by Platt & Munk, Publishers,
a division of Grosset & Dunlap, Inc.,
which is a member of The Putnam Publishing Group, New York.
Published simultaneously in Canada.
Printed in the United States of America.
Library of Congress Catalog Card Number: 86-60758   ISBN 0-448-40090-1
H I J

CONTENTS

CONTENTS

UNCLE WIGGILY'S GREETING

DEAR CHILDREN:

This is a quite different book from any others you may have read about me. In this volume I have some adventures with real children, like yourselves, as well as with my animal friends.

These stories tell of the joyous, funny, exciting and everyday adventures that happen to you girls and boys. There is the story about a toothache, which you may read, or have read to you, when you want to forget the pain. There is a story of a good boy and a freckled girl. And there is a story about a bad boy, but not everyone is allowed to read that.

There is a story for nearly every occasion in the life of a little boy or girl; about the joys of Christmas, of a birthday; about different animals, about getting lost, and one about falling in a mud puddle. And there are stories about having the measles and mumps, and getting over them.

I hope you will like this book as well as you seem to have cared for the other volumes about me. And you will find some beautiful pictures in this book.

Now, as Nurse Jane is calling me, I shall have to hop along. But I hope you will enjoy these stories.

Your friend,

UNCLE WIGGILY LONGEARS.

Uncle Wiggily's Story Book

STORY I

UNCLE WIGGILY'S TOOTHACHE

ONCE upon a time there was a boy who had the toothache. It was not a very large tooth that pained him, and, really, it was quite surprising how such a very large ache got into such a small tooth. At least that is what the boy thought.

"But I'm not going to the dentist and let him pull it!" cried the boy, holding his hand over his mouth. "And I'm not going to let anybody in this house pull it, either! So there!" He ran and hid himself in a corner. Girls aren't that way when they have the toothache—only boys.

"Perhaps the tooth will not need pulling," said Mother, as she looked at the boy and saw how much pain he had.

"That's so!" exclaimed Grandma, who was trying to think of some way in which to help the boy. "Maybe the dentist can make a little hole in your tooth, Sonny, and fill the hole with cement, as the man filled the hole in our sidewalk, and then all your pain will stop."

"No, I'm not going to the dentist! I'm not going, I tell you!" cried Sonny. And I think he stamped his foot on the floor, the least little bit. It may have been that he saw a tack sticking up, and wanted to hammer it down with his shoe. But I am afraid it was a stamp of his foot; and afterward that boy was sorry.

But, anyhow, his tooth kept on aching, and it was the kind called "jumping," for it was worse at one time than another. Sometimes the boy thought the pain jumped from one side of his tongue to the other side, and again it seemed that it leaped away up to the roof of his mouth.

The toothache even seemed to turn somersaults and peppersaults, and once it appeared to jump over backward. But it never completely jumped away, which is what the boy wished it would do.

"You'd better let me take you to the dentist's," said his Mother. "He'll either fix the tooth so it won't ache any more, or he'll take it out, so a new tooth will grow in. And, really, the pain the dentist may cause will only be a little one, and it will be all over in a moment. While your tooth may ache all night."

"No, I'm not going to the dentist! I'm not going!" cried Sonny boy, and then again he acted just as if there were a tack in the carpet that needed hammering down with his foot.

Now it was about this time that Uncle Wiggily Longears, the bunny rabbit gentleman, was hopping from his hollow stump bungalow in the woods to go look for an adventure. But, as yet, Uncle Wiggily knew nothing about the boy with the toothache. That came a little later.

"Are you going to be gone long?" asked Nurse Jane Fuzzy Wuzzy, the muskrat lady housekeeper, of the bunny gentleman.

"Only just long enough to have a nice adventure," answered Mr. Longears, and away he hopped on his red, white and blue striped rheumatism crutch, with his pink, twinkling nose held in front of him like the headlight on a choo-choo train.

Now, as it happened, Uncle Wiggily's hollow stump bungalow was not far from the house where the Toothache Boy lived, though the boy had never seen the rabbit's home. He had often wandered in the woods, almost in front of the bunny's bungalow, but, not having the proper sort of eyes, the boy had never seen Uncle Wiggily. It needs very sharp eyes to see the creatures of the woods and fields, and to find the little houses in which they live.

At any rate the boy had never noticed Uncle Wiggily, though the bunny gentleman had often seen the boy. Many a time when you go through the woods the animal folk look out at and see you, when you never even know they are there.

And pretty soon Uncle Wiggily hopped right past the house where the Toothache Boy lived. And just then, for about the tenth time, Mother was saying:

"You had better let me take you to the dentist and have that toothache stopped, Sonny."

"No! No! I don't want to! I—I'm a—a—I guess it will stop itself," said the boy, hopeful like.

Uncle Wiggily, hiding in the bushes in front of the boy's house, sat up on his hind legs and twinkled his pink nose. By a strange and wonderful new power which he had, the bunny gentleman could hear and understand boy and girl talk, though he could not speak it himself. So it was no trouble at all for Uncle Wiggily to know what that boy was saying.

"He's afraid; that's what the boy is," said the bunny uncle to himself, leaning on his red, white and blue striped crutch. "He's afraid to go to the dentist and have that tooth filled, or pulled. Now that's very silly of him, for the dentist will not hurt him much, and will soon stop the ache. I wonder how I can make that boy believe this? His mother and grandmother can't seem to."

For Mr. Longears heard Mother and Grandma trying to get that Toothache Boy to let them take him to the dentist. But the boy only shook his head, and made believe hammer tacks in the carpet with his foot, and he held his hand over his mouth. But, all the while, the ache kept aching achier and achier and jumping, leaping, tumbling, twisting, turning and flip-flopping —almost like a clown in the circus.

"No! No! I'm not going to the dentist!" cried the boy.

Then Uncle Wiggily had an idea. He could look in through the window of the house and see the boy. In front of the window was a grassy place, near the edge of the wood, and close by was an old stump, shaped almost like the easy chair in a dentist's office.

"I know what I'll do," said Uncle Wiggily. "I'll make believe I have the toothache. I'll go get Dr. Possum and I'll sit down in this stump chair. Then I'll tell Dr. Possum to make believe pull out one of my teeth.

"I s'pose if Nurse Jane were here she might ask what good that would do?" thought Uncle Wiggily. "But I think it will do a lot of good. If that boy sees me, a rabbit gentleman, having a tooth pulled, which is what he will think he sees, it may make him brave enough to go to the dentist's. I'll try it."

Away hopped Uncle Wiggily to Dr. Possum's office.

"What's the matter? Rheumatism again?" asked the animal doctor.

"No, but I want you to come over and pull a tooth for me," said Uncle Wiggily, blinking one eye, and twinkling his pink nose surreptitious-like.

"Pull a tooth! Why, your teeth are all right!" cried Dr. Possum.

"It's to give a little lesson to a boy," whispered the bunny, and then Dr. Possum blinked one eye, in understanding fashion.

A little later Uncle Wiggily sat himself down on the old stump that looked like a chair, and Dr. Possum stood over him.

"Open your mouth and show me which tooth it is that hurts," said Dr. Possum, just like a dentist.

"All right," answered Uncle Wiggily, and, from the corner of his left eye the bunny gentleman could see the Toothache Boy at the window looking out. The boy saw the rabbit and Dr. Possum at the old stump, and he saw Mr. Longears open his mouth and point with his paw to a tooth.

"Oh, Mother!" cried the boy, very much excited. "Look! There's a funny rabbit, all dressed up in a tall silk hat, having a tooth pulled. Grandma, look!"

"Well, I do declare!" murmured the old lady. "Isn't that perfectly wonderful! I didn't know that animals ever had the toothache!"

"Oh, I s'pose they do, once in a while," said the Toothache

Boy's mother.   "But see how brave that rabbit gentleman is! Not to mind having the animal dentist stop his ache!   Just fancy!"

Neither Grandma nor Mother said anything to Sonny Boy. All three of them just stood at the window, and watched Uncle Wiggily and Dr. Possum.   And, as they looked, Dr. Possum put a little shiny thing, like a buttonhook, in the bunny gentleman's mouth.   He gave a sudden little pull and, a moment later, held up something which sparkled in the sun.   It was only a bit of glass, which Uncle Wiggily had held in his paw ready for this part in the little play, but it looked like a tooth.

"Well, I declare!" laughed Grandma.   "The bunny had his tooth pulled!"

"And he doesn't seem to mind it at all," added Mother.

Surely enough, Uncle Wiggily hopped off the make-believe dentist-stump, and with his red, white and blue striped rheumatism crutch, began to dance a little jiggity-jig with Dr. Possum.

"This dance is to show that it doesn't hurt even to have a tooth pulled; much less to have one filled," said the bunny.

"I understand!" laughed Dr. Possum.   And as he and Uncle Wiggily danced, they looked, out of the corners of their eyes, and saw the Toothache Boy standing at the window watching them.

"Well, I never, in all my born days, saw a sight like that!" exclaimed Grandma.

"Nor I," said Mother.   "Isn't it wonderful!"

Sonny Boy took his hand down from his mouth.

"I—I guess, Mother," he said, as he saw Uncle Wiggily

jump over his crutch in a most happy fashion, "I guess I'll go to the dentist, and have him stop my toothache!"

"Hurray!" softly cried Uncle Wiggily, who heard what the boy said. "This is just what I wanted to happen, Dr. Possum! Our little lesson is over. Now we may go!"

Away hopped the bunny, to tell Nurse Jane about the strange adventure, and Dr. Possum, with his bag of powders and pills on his tail, where he always carried it, shuffled back to his office.

Sonny Boy went to the dentist's, and soon his tooth was fixed so it would not ache again. He hardly felt at all what the dentist did to him.

"I—I didn't know how easy it was 'till I saw the rabbit have his tooth pulled," said the boy to the dentist.

"Hum," said the dentist, noncommittal-like, "some rabbits are very funny!"

And if the puppy dog doesn't waggle his tail so hard that he knocks over the milk bottle when it's trying to slide down the door mat, I shall have the pleasure, next, of telling you the story of Uncle Wiggily and the freckled girl.

STORY II

UNCLE WIGGILY AND THE FRECKLED GIRL

UNCLE WIGGILY was hopping through the woods one summer day, when, as he happened to stop to get a drink of some water that the rain-clouds had dropped in the cup of a Jack-in-the-pulpit flower, the bunny gentleman heard a girl saying:

"Oh, I wish I could get them off! I wish I could scrub them off with sandpaper, or something like that! I've tried lemon juice and vinegar, but they won't go. And oh, they make me so homely!"

Uncle Wiggily stopped suddenly and rubbed the end of his pink, twinkling nose with the brim of his tall, silk hat.

"This is very queer," said the bunny uncle to himself. "I wonder what is it she has tried to take off with lemon juice? She seems very unhappy, this little girl does."

The bunny uncle looked through the trees and, seated on a green, mossy stump, he saw a girl about ten or twelve years old. She held a looking-glass in her hand, and as she glanced at her likeness in the mirror she kept saying:

"How can I get them off? How can I make them disappear so I will be beautiful? Oh, how I hate them!"

"What in the world can be the matter?" thought Uncle Wiggily to himself. For, as I have told you, the bunny gentleman was now able to hear and understand the talk of girls and boys, though he could not himself speak that language.

10

He hopped a little closer to the unhappy girl on the green, mossy stump, but the bunny stepped so softly on the leaf carpet of the forest that scarcely a sound did he make, and the girl with the mirror never heard him.

"I wonder if I said a little verse, such as I have read in fairy books, whether they would go away?" murmured the girl. "I've tried everything but that. I'll do it—I'll say a magical verse! But I must make up one, for I never have read of the kind I want in any book."

She seemed to be thinking deeply for a moment and then, shutting her eyes, and looking up at the sun which was shining through the trees of the wood, the girl recited this little verse:

"Sun, sun, who made them come,
Make them go away.
Then I'll be like other girls,
Happy all the day!"

"This is like a puzzle, or a riddle," whispered Uncle Wiggily to himself, as he kept out of sight behind a bush near the stump. "What is it she wants the sun to make go away? It can't be rain, or storm clouds, for the sky is as blue as a baby's eyes. I wonder what it is?"

Then, as the girl took up the mirror again, and looked in it, Uncle Wiggily saw the reflection of her face.

It was covered with dear, little brown freckles!

"Ho! Ho!" softly crooned Uncle Wiggily to himself. "Now I understand. This girl is unhappy because she is freckled. She thinks she doesn't look pretty with them! Why, if she only knew it, those freckles show how strong and healthy she is.   They show that she has played out in the fresh air and sunshine, and that she will live to be happy a long, long while. Freckles! Why, she ought to be glad she has them, instead of sorry!"

But the girl on the stump kept her eyes shut, clenching the mirror in her hand and as she held her face up to the sun she recited another verse of what she thought was a mystic charm.

This is what she said:

"Freckles, freckles, go away!
Don't come back any other day.
Make my face most fair to see,
Then how happy I will be!"

Slowly, as Uncle Wiggily watched, hidden as he was behind the bush, the girl opened her eyes and held up the looking-glass. Over her shoulder the bunny gentleman could still see the freckles in the glass; the dear, brown, honest, healthy freckles. But when the girl saw them she dropped the mirror, hid her face in her hands and cried:

"Oh, they didn't go 'way! They didn't go 'way! Now I never can be beautiful!"

Uncle Wiggily twinkled his pink nose thoughtfully.

"This is too bad!" said the bunny gentleman. "I wonder how I can help that girl?" For, since he had helped the Tooth-ache Boy by letting Dr. Possum pretend to pull an aching tooth, the bunny gentleman wanted do other favors for the children who loved him.

"I'd like to make that girl happy, even with her freckles,"

said the bunny. "I'll hop off through the woods, and perhaps I may meet some of my animal friends who will show me a way."

The bunny gentleman looked kindly at the girl on the stump. She was sobbing, and did not see him, or hear him, as she murmured over and over again:

"I don't like freckles! I hate them!"

Away through the woods hopped Uncle Wiggily. He had not gone very far before he heard a bird singing a beautiful song. Oh, so cheerful it was, and happy—that song!

"Good morning, Mr. Bird!" greeted Uncle Wiggily, for you know it is the father bird who sings the sweetest song. The mother bird is so busy, I suppose, that she has little time to sing. "You are very happy this morning," the rabbit said to the bird.

"Why, yes, Uncle Wiggily, I am very happy," answered Mr. Bird, "and so is my wife. She is up there on the nest, but she told me to come down here and sing a happy song."

"Why?" asked the bunny.

"Because we are going to have some little birds," was the answer. "There are some eggs in our nest, and my mate is sitting on them to keep them warm. Soon some little birds will come out, and I will sing a still happier song."

"That's fine," said Uncle Wiggily, thinking of the unhappy freckled girl on the stump. "May I see the eggs in your nest?"

"Of course," answered the father-singer. "Our nest is in a low bush, but it is well hidden. Here, I'll show you. Mrs. Bird will not mind if you look."

The father bird fluttered to the nest, and Mrs. Bird raised

her fluffy feathers to show Uncle Wiggily some beautiful blue eggs.

"Why—why, they're *freckled!*" exclaimed the bunny gentleman. "Aren't you birds sad because you have freckled eggs? Why, your little birds will be freckled, too! And, if they are girl birds they will cry!"

"Why?" asked Mr. Bird in surprise. "Why will our girl birdies cry?"

"Because they'll be *freckled*," answered the bunny. "I just saw a girl in the woods, crying to break her heart because she is freckled!"

"Nonsense!" chirped Mrs. Bird. "In the first place these are not freckles on my eggs, though they look so. My eggs are spotted, or mottled, and they would not be half so pretty if they were not colored that way. Besides, being spotted as they are, makes them not so easily seen in the nest. And, when I fly away to get food, bad snakes or cats can not so easily see my eggs to eat them. I just love my *freckled* eggs, as you call them!" laughed Mrs. Bird.

"Well, they are pretty," admitted Uncle Wiggily. "But will your little birds be speckled, too?"

"Not at all," sang Mr. Bird. "Say, Uncle Wiggily!" he whistled, "if we could get that girl here so she could see our spotted eggs, and know how beautiful they are, even if they are what she would call 'freckled'; wouldn't that make her happier?"

"Perhaps it would," said the bunny rabbit. "I never thought of that. I'll try it! You will not be afraid to let her see your eggs, will you?" he asked.

"No; for girls are not like some boys—they don't rob the nests of birds," replied the mother of the speckled eggs. "Bring the unhappy girl here, and Mr. Bird and I will hide in the bushes while she peeps into our nest."

"I will!" said Uncle Wiggily.

Away he hopped through the woods, and soon he came to the place where the freckled girl was still sobbing on the stump.

"Now how can I get her to follow me through the woods, to see the nest, when I can't talk to her?" whispered Uncle Wiggily.

Then he thought of a plan.

"I'll toss a little piece of tree-bark at her," chuckled the bunny. "That will make her look up, and when she sees me I'll hop off a little way. She'll follow, thinking she can catch me. But I'll keep ahead of her and so lead her to the woods. I want to make her happy!"

The bunny tossed a bit of bark, hitting the girl on her head. She looked around, and then she saw Uncle Wiggily, all dressed up as he was with his tall silk hat and his red, white and blue striped rheumatism crutch.

"Oh, what a funny rabbit!" exclaimed the girl, smiling through her tears, and forgetting her freckles, for a while at least. "I wonder if I can catch you?" she said.

"Well, not if I know it," whispered Uncle Wiggily to himself, for he knew what the girl had said. "But I'll let you think you can," the bunny chuckled to himself.

He hopped on a little farther, and the girl followed. But just as she thought she was going to put her hands on the rabbit, Uncle Wiggily skipped along, and she missed him. But still she followed on, and soon Uncle Wiggily had led her to the bushes where the birds had built their nest.

Mr. and Mrs. Bird were watching, and when they saw Uncle Wiggily and the freckled girl, Mr. Bird began to sing. He sang of blue skies, or rippling waters of sunshine and sweet breezes scented with apple blossoms.

"Oh, what a lovely song!" murmured the freckled girl. "Some birds must live here. I wonder if I could see their nest and eggs? I wouldn't hurt them for the world!" she said softly.

Uncle Wiggily shrank back out of sight. The girl looked around for the singing birds, and just then the wind blew aside some leaves and she saw the nest. But she saw more than the nest, for she saw the eggs that were to be hatched into little birds. And, more than this; the girl saw that the eggs were spotted or mottled—freckled as she was herself!

"Oh! Oh!" murmured the girl, clasping her hands as she looked down at the speckled eggs in the nest. "They have brown spots on, just like my face. They are *freckled eggs*— but, oh, how pretty they are! I never knew that anything freckled could be beautiful! I never knew! Oh, how wonderful!"

As she stood looking at the eggs, Mr. Bird sang again, a sweeter song than before, and the wind blew softly on the freckled face of the unhappy girl—no, not unhappy now, for she smiled, and there were no more tears in her eyes.

"Oh, how glad I am that the funny rabbit led me to the nest of freckled eggs!" said the girl. "I wonder where he is?"

She looked around, but Uncle Wiggily had hopped away. He had done all that was needed of him.

The mother bird softly fluttered down into her nest, covering the beautiful mottled eggs with her downy wings. She was not afraid of the girl. The girl reached out her hand and timidly stroked the mother bird. Then she gently touched her own freckled cheeks.

"I'm never going to care any more," she whispered. "I did not know that freckles could be so pretty. I'm glad I got 'em!"

The freckled girl walked away, leaving the mother bird on the nest, while the father of the speckled eggs, that soon would be little birds, sang his song of joy. The freckled girl, with a glad smile on her face, went back to the stump, and, without looking into the mirror, she tossed the bit of looking-glass into a deep spring.

"I don't need you any more," she said, as the glass went sailing through the air. "I know, now, that freckles can be beautiful!"

And if the pussy cat doesn't think the automobile tire is a bologna sausage, and try to nibble a piece out to make a sandwich for the rag doll's picnic, I'll tell you next about Uncle Wiggily and the mud puddle.

STORY III

UNCLE WIGGILY AND THE MUD PUDDLE

Did you ever fall down in a mud puddle? Perhaps this may have happened to you when you were barefooted, with old clothes on, so that it did not much matter whether you splashed them or not.

But that isn't what I mean.

Did you ever fall into a mud puddle when you had on your very best clothes, with white stockings that showed every speck of mud? If anything like that ever happened to you, when you were going to Sunday-school, or to a little afternoon tea party, why, you know how dreadfully unhappy you felt! To say nothing of the pain in your knees!

Well, now for a story of how a little boy named Tommie fell in a mud puddle, and how Uncle Wiggily helped him scrub the mud off his white stockings—off Tommie's white stockings I mean, not Uncle Wiggily's.

Tommie was a little boy who lived in a house on the edge of the wood, near where Uncle Wiggily had built his hollow stump bungalow. No, Tommie wasn't the same little boy who had the toothache. He was quite a different chap.

One day the postman rang the bell at Tommie's house, and gave Tommie a cute little letter.

"Oh, it's for me!" cried Tommie. "Look, Mother! I have a letter!"

18

"That's nice," said Mother. "Who sent it to you?"

"I'll look and tell you," answered the little boy. The writing in the letter was large and plain, and though Tommie had not been to school very long he could read a little. So he was able to tell that the letter was from a little girl named Alice, who wanted him to come to a party she was going to have one afternoon a few days later.

"Oh, may I go?" Tommie asked his mother.

"Yes," she answered.

"And wear my best clothes?"

"Surely you will put on your best clothes to go to the party," said Mother. "And I hope you have a nice time!"

Tommie hoped so, too. But if only he had known what was going to happen! Perhaps it is just as well he did not, for it would have spoiled his fun of thinking about the coming party. And half the fun of nearly everything, you know, is thinking about it beforehand, or afterward.

At last the day came for the tea party Alice was to give at her home, which was a little distance down the street from Tommie's house.

"Oh, how happy I am!" sang Tommie, as he ran about the porch.

But when, after breakfast, it began to rain, Tommie was not so happy. He stood with his nose pressed against the glass of the window until it was pressed quite flat. I mean his nose was flat, for the glass was that way anyhow, you know. And Tommie watched the rain drops splash down, making little mud puddles in the street.

"Can't I go to Alice's party if it rains?" asked Tommie.

"Well, no, I think not," Mother answered. "But perhaps it will stop raining before it is time for you to go. You don't have to leave here until after lunch."

Tommie turned again to press his nose against the glass, glad that the rain was outside, so that the drops which rolled down the window could not wet his face. And he hoped the clouds would clear away and that the sun would shine before the time for the party.

Now about this same hour Uncle Wiggily Longears, the bunny rabbit gentleman, was also looking out of the window of his hollow stump bungalow in the woods, wondering, just as Tommie wondered, whether the rain would stop.

"But surely you won't go out while it is still raining," said Nurse Jane Fuzzy Wuzzy, the muskrat lady housekeeper.

"No," answered Uncle Wiggily, "my going out is not so needful as all that. I was going to look for an adventure, and I had rather do that in the sunshine than in the rain. I can wait."

And then, almost as suddenly as it had started, the rain stopped.

"Oh, I'm so glad!" sang Tommie, as he danced up and down. "Now I can go to the party!"

"And I can go adventuring," said Uncle Wiggily. Now of course he did not hear Tommie, nor did the little boy hear the bunny. But, all the same, they were to have an adventure together.

Tommie had been ready, for some time, to start down the street to go to the party Alice was giving for her little girl and boy friends. All that Tommie needed, now, was to have his collar and tie put on, and his hair combed again, for it had become rather tossed and twisted topsy-turvy when he pressed his head against the window, watching the rain.

"Be careful of mud puddles!" Tommie's mother called to him, as, all spick and span, he started down the street toward the home of Alice, a block or so distant. "Don't fall in any puddles!"

"I'll be careful," Tommie promised.

And as Uncle Wiggily started out about this same time for his adventure, Nurse Jane called to the bunny:

"Be careful not to get wet on account of your rheumatism."

"I'll be careful," promised Uncle Wiggily, just as Tommie had done.

Now everything would have been all right if Tommie had not stubbed his toe as he was going along the street, about half way to the party. But he did stumble, where one sidewalk stone was raised up higher than another, and, before he could save himself, down in the mud puddle fell poor Tommie! He fell on his hands and knees, and they were both soaked in the muddy water of the puddle on the sidewalk.

Of course it did not so much matter about Tommie's hands. He could easily wash the mud and brown water off them. But it was different with his white stockings. Perhaps I forgot to tell you that Tommie wore white stockings to the party. But he did, and now the knees of these stockings were all mud!

And as he looked at his mud-soiled stockings, and at his hands, from which water was dripping down on the sides of his legs, Tommie could not help crying.

"I can't go to the party this way!" sobbed Tommie to himself, for he was big enough to go down the street alone, and there were no other children on it just then. "I can't go to the party this way! But if I go home Mother will make me change my things, and I'll be late, and maybe she won't let me go at all! Oh, dear!"

And in order to keep out of sight of any other boys or girls who might come along, Tommie stepped behind some bushes that grew along the street.

He looked down at his mud soiled stockings

And what was his surprise to see, sitting on a stone, behind this same bush, an old gentleman rabbit, wearing glasses, and with a tall silk hat on his head. On the ground beside him was a red, white and blue striped crutch, for rheumatism.

But the funniest thing about the rabbit gentleman (who,

as you have guessed, was Uncle Wiggily), the funniest thing was that he had a bunch of dried grass in one paw, and he was busy scrubbing some dried spots of mud off his trousers. So busy was Uncle Wiggily doing this that he neither saw nor heard Tommie come behind the bush. And Tommie was so surprised at seeing Uncle Wiggily that the little boy never said a word.

"Why—why!" thought Tommie, as he saw the bunny take up a pine tree cone, which was like a nutmeg grater, and scrape the dried mud off his trousers, "he must have fallen into a mud puddle just as I did!"

And that is just what had happened to Uncle Wiggily. He had been walking along, thinking of an adventure he might have, when he splashed into a puddle and spattered himself with mud!

But, instead of crying, Uncle Wiggily set about making the best of it—cleaning himself off so he would look nice again, to go in search of an adventure.

"I'll let the mud dry in the sun," said Uncle Wiggily out loud, speaking to himself, with his back partly turned to Tommie. "Then it will easily scrape off."

The sun was so warm, after the rain, that it soon dried the mud on the bunny gentleman's clothes, and with the bunch of grass, and the sharp pine tree cone, he soon had loosened the bits of dirt.

"Now I'm all right again," said Uncle Wiggily out loud. And though of course Tommie did not understand rabbit talk, the little boy could see what Uncle Wiggily had done to help himself after the mud-puddle accident.

"I say!" cried Tommie, before he thought, "will you please lend me that pine tree cone clothes brush? I want to clean the mud off my white stockings so I can go to the party!"

Uncle Wiggily looked up in surprise! He had not known, before, that Tommie was there; but the bunny heard what the little boy said. With a low and polite bow of his tall silk hat, Uncle Wiggily tossed the bunch of grass and the pine cone to Tommie. By that time the mud had dried so the little boy could scrape most of it off his stockings.

"I hope you have a nice time at the party," said Uncle Wiggily, in rabbit language, of course. And then, as Tommie scraped the last of the dried mud away, leaving only a few spots on his stockings, the bunny gentleman hopped out of the bush and on his way.

"And I can go to Alice's house without having to run home to change my stockings," thought Tommie. "I wonder who that rabbit was?"

And when Tommie reached the party he found that he was not the only little boy who had fallen in a mud puddle. The same thing had happened to Sammie and Johnnie, two other boys.

"But how did you get your stockings so clean, without going home and changing them?" asked the other boys of Tommie.

"Oh, an old rabbit gentleman, with a tall silk hat and a red, white and blue crutch showed me how to scrape off the dried mud with a pine cone," Tommie answered. "I cleaned my white stockings as the bunny brushed his clothes."

"Oh, is that a fairy story?" cried the boys and girls at Alice's party.

"Well, he *looked* like a fairy!" laughed Tommie, who had washed his hands in the bath room at Alice's house, so they were clean for eating cake and ice cream. "And I'm not afraid of mud puddles any more. I know what to do if I fall in one," said Tommie.

And if the onion doesn't make tears come into the eyes of the potato when they're playing tag around the spoon in the soup dish, the next story will be about Uncle Wiggily and the bad boy.

STORY IV

UNCLE WIGGILY AND THE BAD BOY

ONCE upon a time there was a bad boy. He lived on the edge of the wood in which Uncle Wiggily Longears, the bunny rabbit gentleman, had built his hollow stump bungalow. The bad boy did not know Uncle Wiggily, but Mr. Longears knew about the bad boy, and so did Nurse Jane Fuzzy Wuzzy, the bunny's muskrat lady housekeeper.

"Don't ever go near that bad boy's house," said Miss Fuzzy Wuzzy one morning, as the rabbit gentleman started out with his red, white and blue striped rheumatism crutch.

"Why not?" asked Uncle Wiggily.

"Because," answered Miss Fuzzy Wuzzy, "that boy will throw stones at you, and maybe hit you on your pink, twinkling nose."

"He can't throw stones now," said Uncle Wiggily. "He can't find any. The ground is covered with snow."

"Then he'll throw snowballs at you," said the muskrat lady housekeeper. "Please keep away from him."

"I'll think about it," promised the bunny gentleman, as he hopped away, with his tall, silk hat on his head.

Now you know why, once upon a time, there was a bad boy. He was bad because he threw stones and snowballs at rabbits and other animals. There were more things bad about him than this, but one is enough for a story.

26

Uncle Wiggily hopped on and on, across the fields and through the woods, and soon he came to the house of the bad boy. It was a regular house, not a hollow stump bungalow, such as that in which Mr. Longears lived.

"I wonder if there isn't any way of making that bad boy good?" thought the bunny rabbit gentleman. "Bad boys aren't of much use in the world, but good boys, or girls, who put out crumbs for the hungry birds to eat in winter—they are of great use in the world! I wonder if I could make that bad boy good?"

But, no sooner had Uncle Wiggily began to wonder in this fashion, than, all of a sudden, he heard a loud voice shouting:

"Hi! There he is! A rabbit! I'm going to throw a snowball at him!"

Uncle Wiggily looked over his shoulder and saw the bad boy rushing out of his house, followed by another boy.

"Oh, what a nice, funny rabbit!" cried the second boy. "He looks as if he came from a circus—all dressed up!"

"I'll make him turn a somersault if I can whang him with a snowball!" shouted the bad boy, running toward the bunny gentleman.

"Perhaps I had better be going," said Uncle Wiggily, who could understand boy and girl talk, though he could not speak it himself. "I'll wait until some other day about trying to make this boy good."

Mr. Longears started to run, but he had not taken many hops before, all of a sudden, he felt a sharp, thumping pain in his side, and he was almost knocked over by a snowball thrown by the bad boy.

"Hi there! I hit him! I hit him!" howled the bad boy, dancing up and down.

"Yes," sadly said the other chap. "You hit him, but what good did it do?"

"It shows I'm a straight shot!" proudly answered the other. "Maybe I can catch that rabbit now."

He ran over the snow. But though Uncle Wiggily had been knocked down by the ball thrown by the bad boy, the rabbit gentleman managed to get to his feet, and away he hopped on his rheumatism crutch—so fast that the bad boy could not get him.

Then the bad boy and the other chap, who was not so bad, played in the snow, until it was time to go home. Uncle Wiggily hopped to his hollow stump bungalow, but he said nothing to Nurse Jane about the pain in his side.

"If I tell her she won't let me go out to the movies to-night with Grandpa Goosey," thought Mr. Longears.

So, though his side pained him, Uncle Wiggily said never a word, but early that evening he hopped over to Grandpa Goosey's home in the duck pen. And on the way Uncle Wiggily had to pass the house of the bad boy.

"But it is getting dark, and he will not see me," thought the bunny gentleman. "I guess it will be safe."

Now it happened that, just as Uncle Wiggily was hopping under the window of the bad boy's house, the bunny heard a voice inside saying:

"Oh, dear! How my ear aches! Oh, what a pain! Can't you do something to stop it, Mother?"

"If I had some soft cotton I could put a little warm oil on it and that, in your ear, would make it feel better," answered a lady's voice. "But I have no cotton in the house. If you'll wait until I go to the drug store——"

"No! No!" howled the voice of the bad boy. "I don't want you to go to the store and leave me alone! Can't you get some cotton without going to the store?"

"No," answered the mother. "You shouldn't have played out in the cold, and thrown snowballs at the rabbit. You must have gotten some snow in your ear to make it ache!"

"Oh, do something to make it stop!" cried the bad boy. "Oh, why haven't we some cotton?"

Uncle Wiggily, outside under the window, heard all this talk. Now the bunny gentleman knew where to find something like cotton without going to the drug store. Inside each of the big brown buds of the horse-chestnut tree is a little wad of cotton. Mother Nature puts the cotton there to keep the bud warm through the winter, so green leaves will come out in the spring.

Uncle Wiggily looked around and saw, lying on the snow, a branch which the wind had broken from a horse-chestnut tree. Hopping across the newly-fallen spring snow to this branch, Uncle Wiggily gnawed off some of the buds. Breaking these open with his teeth, he took out some of the soft, fluffy cotton.

"I'll just leave this on the bad boy's doorstep," thought the bunny. "I'll tap with my crutch and hop away."

So the bunny gentleman, with the wad of cotton, skipped up the front steps of the house when no one saw him. His paws made funny little marks in the soft snow. Uncle Wiggily put the cotton on the sill, tapped once, twice, three times with his rheumatism crutch, and then hopped away.

"Somebody's at the door!" said the bad boy. "Maybe that's daddy coming home, so he can go to the drug store and get that cotton for my aching ear."

"Maybe," said his mother. "I hope it is."

She opened the door, and when she saw there the bunch of cotton—just what she wanted—you can imagine how surprised she was!

"Why, who could have left it?" asked the bad boy, when his mother told him what had happened. "Who do you s'pose did?"

"I don't know," she answered. "But I saw some rabbit tracks in the snow on our steps."

"Rabbit tracks?" repeated the boy, wonderingly, as his mother softly put some warm cotton and oil in his ear, making the pain almost stop.

"Yes, rabbit tracks," said Mother. "And, if I were you, I'd never throw any more snowballs at rabbits."

The boy (I'll not call him bad any more) put his head down on the pillow of his bed. He could go to sleep now, as the pain in his ear had almost stopped.

"I wonder if that funny rabbit, dressed up like a little old man, could have brought me the cotton?" said the boy.

"I wonder, too," softly spoke Mother with a smile.

"Anyhow, I won't ever throw stones or snowballs at rabbits any more," promised the boy.

"Or cats or dogs, either?" his mother asked.

"Or cats or dogs, either," added the boy.

Then he went to sleep, and Uncle Wiggily, picking the bits of fuzzy horse-chestnut tree cotton off his tall, silk hat, hopped on to Grandpa Goosey's house and went to the movies.

So that's the story of the bunny gentleman and the bad boy, and I hope you liked it. But if the rag doll's go-cart doesn't race with the baby carriage and slip on the banana skin as though it had on roller skates, I'll tell you in the next story about Uncle Wiggily and the good boy.

STORY V

UNCLE WIGGILY AND THE GOOD BOY

"Now do be careful to-day, please, Uncle Wiggily," begged Nurse Jane Fuzzy Wuzzy, the muskrat lady housekeeper of the bunny rabbit gentleman, as he hopped down off the steps of his hollow stump bungalow one morning.

"Now do be careful today."

"Careful? Why, I'm always careful," answered the bunny, as he twinkled one side of his pink nose and looked to make sure that his red, white and blue striped rheumatism crutch was not painted green. "Don't you think so, Nurse Jane?" asked Mr. Longears.

"Indeed I do not," Miss Fuzzy Wuzzy answered. "You get so excited, looking for adventures, that you don't care whether you are chased by the Pipsisewah or Skeezicks."

"But I always get away from them; don't I?" asked Uncle Wiggily. "And the Woozie Wolf, the Fuzzy Fox and even the Skillery Scallery Alligator. I always get away, Nurse Jane."

"It is hard work for you, sometimes," said the muskrat lady. "I do wish you would be more careful, Wiggy. Besides, these new adventures of yours—helping real girls and boys out of their troubles—are dangerous. Of course, I love children, and I know you do, also. But some day you'll be caught by one of these bad boys or girls."

"There aren't any bad girls," laughed Uncle Wiggily. "They are just a bit funny; that's all. As for bad boys; well, I hope to see them all turn good. And, anyhow, the children love me so much I don't believe they'll harm me."

"Well, you'd better be careful just the same," Nurse Jane said. Then she went in to dust the dishes and sweep the furniture, and Uncle Wiggily hopped over the fields and through the woods, looking for an adventure.

The bunny gentleman had not gone far from his hollow stump bungalow before he saw a crowd of boys on their way to school. One of the boys had a tin can in his hand, and another carried a piece of rope.

"Oh, maybe those boys are going camping," thought Uncle Wiggily, "and they're going to build a campfire and cook their carrot soup, or whatever they eat, in the tin can over the fire. I'll hide in the bushes and watch them. And I can hear what they say."

By means of a gift which a good fairy gave him, Uncle Wiggily, for a time, was able to hear and understand the talk of boys and girls, though he could not, himself, speak their language. He wanted to hear what these boys would say, so the bunny gentleman hid in the bushes.

The boys came along, laughing, shouting and trying to sing, but that last they did not do as well as girls would have done. Somehow or other, girls are better singers than boys.

Well, anyhow, the boys came nearer to where Uncle Wiggily was hiding in the bushes, and, all of a sudden, one of the lads gave a whoop like a wild Indian, and cried:

"There's a dog! Let's get him!"

"There, now!" thought Uncle Wiggily to himself. "I knew boys were good. They want to take that dog with them to camp and give him some of the soup they are going to boil in the tin can. I hope they don't give it to him too hot, though, and burn his tongue."

Uncle Wiggily peeked over the top of the bush, and saw one of the boys chasing the dog. It was a little dog; rather thin, so you could almost count his ribs, and he did not seem to have had much to eat of late. And as soon as the dog saw the boy running after him, that dog began to run also.

"Why, that's queer," said Uncle Wiggily. "Why does the dog run away from that good boy? If I were only nearer I'd tell the dog that the boy is going to be kind to him and give him tomato-can camp-soup."

"Oh, let the dog go!" called a red-haired boy to the one who was running along with the tin can in his hand.

"No, I'm going to catch him and tie this tin can on his tail," the first boy answered. "You ought to see how fast he'll run when he has this tin can on his tail!"

"Dear me!" thought Uncle Wiggily, hardly able to believe what he heard. "Tie a tin can on a dog's tail! And I thought that boy was going to be kind! Oh, oh, what a mistake I made!"

Most of the boys turned off on another path and went to school, but the one with the tin can chased after the dog, and another boy, who seemed very nice and quiet, stayed near the bush, behind which Uncle Wiggily was hidden. Finally the boy with the tin can caught the poor, thin, yelping dog, and carried him back to the bush.

"Where's that piece of rope?" asked the bad boy, holding the yelping, squirming little dog under one arm, while in the other hand he carried the empty tin can.

"What are you going to do with the rope?" asked the quiet boy. He held his hands behind his back.

"I'm going to use the rope to tie this tin can on the dog's tail," answered the bad boy. "That's what I am!"

"Then I won't give to to you," spoke the quiet lad. "I'm not going to let you tie any tin can to a dog's tail if I can help it! There! You can't have the rope!"

With a sudden motion he threw, away over in the weeds, the rope, which he had picked up after another lad had dropped it to go to school.

"Oh, ho! So that's what you're going to do, is it?" cried the bad boy. "I'll fix you for that!"

He dropped his tin can; but still holding the poor dog under his arm, the bad boy rushed at the quiet chap.

"I'll make you get that rope and help me tie the tin can on this dog's tail!" cried the bad boy.

"I think it is about time for me to do something," said Uncle Wiggily to himself. The bunny gentleman, hidden behind the bush, had heard all that was said.

All of a sudden, just as the bad boy was going to hit the quiet lad, for not helping to tie the tin can on the dog's tail, Uncle Wiggily turned, and, in the soft sand and dirt, began to dig very fast with his paws.

Now a rabbit gentleman is one of the best diggers in the world. With his paws he can make himself a burrow, or underground house, almost before you can eat a lollypop. And Uncle Wiggily, pawing in the dirt, made a regular shower of sand, gravel and little stones fly right in the face of the bad boy.

By looking over his shoulder Uncle Wiggily could see which way to dig so that the sand would go in the eyes of the bad boy, but not in the face of the one who was kind to animals.

"Whiff! Whiff! Whiff! the sand, gravel and little stones shot over the top of the bushes, and spattered all over the bad boy.

"Say! Who's doing that?" cried the unkind chap, trying to hold his arm in front of his face to keep the sand out of his eyes. "If you fellows don't stop that——"

But he couldn't say any more, for a lot of sand went flying into his mouth. He dropped the poor, thin dog, who ran away and hid himself in a hollow tree. and then the bad boy had to use both hands to wipe out the gravel that rattled down inside his shirt, and so he couldn't hit the kind boy.

"Who's scattering that gravel?" cried the bad boy, scowling.

"I don't see anyone," said the other, smiling.

But there was Uncle Wiggily, behind the bush, scattering the gravel with his paws in a regular shower.

"I wish Nurse Jane could see me now," chuckled the bunny gentleman. "She surely would laugh."

At last so much gravel, sand and little stones showered into the face of the bad boy that he ran away, crying:

"Oh! Oh! Oh! Something terrible must have happened! I guess I'd better not tie any tin cans on dogs' tails any more."

"I guess you'd better not," said the other boy.

"And I say the same," laughed Uncle Wiggily, as he brushed some dust off his tall, silk hat, and straightened his necktie. Then the bunny gentleman watched, while the kind boy went to the hollow tree and patted the poor, frightened little dog. And then this boy hid the tin can where no other boys could find it, and went on to school.

And I think—mind you I'm not sure—but I think that bad boy turned good after that. Anyhow if he didn't he ought to.

"Well, I had quite an adventure," said the bunny rabbit gentleman, as he hopped on to his hollow stump bungalow. "A very good adventure!"

And if the jumping jack doesn't cut a slice off the mud pie with the bread knife, and tell the rag doll it's a piece of chocolate cake, I'll tell you next about Uncle Wiggily's valentine.

STORY VI

UNCLE WIGGILY'S VALENTINE

UNCLE WIGGILY quickly hopped across the room and closed the door of his hollow stump bungalow, where he was busy in the sitting room. He heard Nurse Jane Fuzzy Wuzzy coming along.

"Well, that's queer!" exclaimed the muskrat lady housekeeper, as she noticed what Uncle Wiggily did. "I wonder what he means? Wiggy," she called, "are you getting ready for some strange, new adventure, such as stopping bad boys from tying tin cans on dogs' tails?"

"Nothing like that now; no, my dear," answered the bunny rabbit, and he quickly pulled the table cover over something he had been looking at. "This is a secret!"

"Oh—a secret!" exclaimed Nurse Jane, puzzled-like.

The muskrat lady looked at a calendar hanging on the wall, and noticed that the day was February 14.

"I think I can guess what your secret is, Uncle Wiggily," she said to herself. "I s'pose it's something for Mrs. Twistytail, the pig lady, or maybe for Grandpa Goosey Gander. Well, I hope you enjoy it."

Then Nurse Jane went back to the dining room, where she was giving the dishes their morning bath; and Uncle Wiggily began to rustle some paper and tie knots in a piece of gold string, the while murmuring to himself:

"I hope she likes it! Oh, I do hope she likes it. I'll put it on the steps, throw a stone at the door so she thinks someone is knocking, and then I'll run and hide behind a bush and watch how surprised she is when she opens it."

Uncle Wiggily had been very busy all that morning, after having been out in the woods the day before. What he had made I shall tell you about in a little while. Enough now for you to know that the bunny rabbit had something he did not want Nurse Jane to see.

Pretty soon, after opening the door a crack, and listening to Miss Fuzzy Wuzzy wash the face of the clock, Uncle Wiggily hopped softly out and down the front steps, with a box under his paw. His tall silk hat was on rather sideways, and he carried his red, white and blue striped rheumatism crutch upside down, but when you remember that it was February 14, I think you will kindly excuse the bunny gentleman.

Uncle Wiggily hopped on through the woods, and over the fields. Every now and then he would stop, and, with his crutch, brush to one side the dried leaves and little heaps of snow that were scattered here and there in the forest.

"I hope I may find some," said Mr. Longears to himself. "It won't be half so pretty without them. I hope I find some."

He searched in many places, and at last he found what he was looking for. Carefully he picked something up off the ground, and put it in the box he carried.

"Nurse Jane will surely like this," said the bunny gentleman. He was about to hop on again when, all of a sudden, he heard someone crying in the woods. There was a sobbing sound and, looking around the corner of a tree, Uncle Wiggily saw a little girl, sitting on a log. And she was crying as hard as she could cry!

"That isn't the Freckled Girl," said the bunny gentleman to himself. "She said she wouldn't mind her freckles after she looked at the pretty speckled birds' eggs. It isn't the Freckled Girl. I wonder who she is, and what's the matter?"

And pretty soon Uncle Wiggily found out, for he heard the sobbing girl say:

"Oh, I wish I had money enough to buy one! All the other girls and boys can buy valentines to send teacher, but I can't! And she'll think I don't like her, but I do! Oh, I wish I had a valentine!"

"My goodness me sakes alive and some peanut pudding!" whispered the bunny rabbit gentleman. "That girl is crying because she hasn't a valentine for her teacher!"

Then the bunny gentleman looked down at the box, wrapped in tissue paper, which he carried under his paw—the box in which he had placed something he had found under the leaves and snow of the forest a little while before.

"She wants a valentine," murmured the bunny rabbit gentleman. "And here I have one that I made for Nurse Jane. I was going to leave it on the steps and surprise my muskrat lady housekeeper. But I suppose I could give it to this little girl, and—well, Nurse Jane won't care, when I tell her.

"I'll do it! I'll give this girl my valentine," said Uncle Wiggily so suddenly that his pink nose almost twinkled backward.

He looked over the top of a bush behind which he had sat down to wrap up Nurse Jane's valentine. Then the bunny hopped over to the girl who sat on the log, still sobbing because she had no token for her teacher.

The girl heard the rustling in the leaves, made by Uncle Wiggily's paws as he hopped, and she looked up suddenly. Then she rubbed her eyes, hardly able to believe what she saw.

"Why! Why!" she murmured. "Am I dreaming? Is this a fairy? A rabbit gentleman, dressed in a tall silk hat, and with his red, white and blue striped rheumatism crutch! Oh! Why, it's Uncle Wiggily! It's Uncle Wiggily out of my Bedtime Story Books! Oh, how glad I am to see you, dear Uncle Wiggily! Please come up and sit by me on this log!"

But Uncle Wiggily was not allowed to do this. He put his paw over his lips, to show that though he could hear, and understand what the girl said, he could not talk to her in reply. Then he placed his valentine beside her on the log and quickly hopped away.

"Oh, Uncle Wiggily! Wait a minute! Please wait a minute!" cried the girl, but the bunny gentleman dared not stay.

"I must try and find Nurse Jane another valentine," he said to himself, as he skipped along the woodland paths.

Left alone, the girl on the log opened the box Uncle Wiggily had left. It was made from pieces of white birch bark, such as the Indians used for their canoes. Inside, were some sprigs from an evergreen tree, with some round, brown buttons from the sycamore tree. And in the middle of the evergreen sprigs were some lovely pink and white blossoms of the trailing arbutus—the earliest flower of Spring—growing under the leaves and late snows. It was these arbutus flowers which the bunny had come to the woods to find and complete his valentine. Now he had given it to the girl.

"Oh, how lovely!" she murmured, tears no longer in her eyes. "Won't teacher be surprised when I put this on her desk and tell her Uncle Wiggily gave it to me? Oh, there's a verse, too!"

And there was! Written on a piece of white birch bark, which is what the animal folk use instead of paper, was this little verse:

> "These twigs of cedar, like my heart,
>   Are ever green for you.
> The blossoms whisper that I am
>   Your Valentine so true!"

"I know teacher will just love this!" said the little girl, and she was so excited she could hardly run to school. She had to hop and skip.

"Here's a valentine Uncle Wiggily gave me in the woods," the little girl told her teacher, all excited and out of breath.

"Uncle Wiggily? How strange!" exclaimed the teacher. "I—I hope you didn't dream it," she said to the little girl. "But, at any rate, the valentine is real. And how lovely! It's the very nicest one I ever saw!"

Then you can imagine how pleased the little girl was. Uncle Wiggily, hopping back to his bungalow through the woods, gnawed a piece of white birch bark off a tree, and, with a burned, black stick for a pencil, he scribbled on it:

"Dear Nurse Jane: This is my valentine. I love you!
                                   "UNCLE WIGGILY."

And when the muskrat lady found that on the doorstep a little later, she laughed and said it was the nicest valentine she could wish for. And when Uncle Wiggily told about giving the other valentine to the sad little girl, the muskrat lady said:

"You did just right, Wiggy! Now let's go to the movies!"

So they did. And if electric light doesn't cry when it has to go down cellar in the dark, to get a piece of coal for the fire to play with, you shall next hear about Uncle Wiggily and the bad dog.

STORY VII

UNCLE WIGGILY AND THE BAD DOG

ONCE upon a time, about as many years ago as it takes a lollypop to slide down the back cellar door, there lived in a kennel, not far from Uncle Wiggily's hollow stump bungalow, a bad dog. And the bunny rabbit gentleman, more than once, wished that this dog would always stay in his kennel, or remain chained in front of it so he couldn't get loose.

"For that dog," said Uncle Wiggily to Nurse Jane Fuzzy Wuzzy, "is the pest of my life! Every time he sees me he chases me. He isn't at all like Jackie and Peetie Bow Wow, or Old Dog Percival."

"Why don't you scratch sand and gravel in his eyes as you did in the face of the bad boy?" asked the muskrat lady housekeeper.

"You can't treat dogs as you do boys," replied Uncle Wiggily. "Though, of course, some boys and some dogs are great friends. But this dog seems always to want to chase me."

"Then you must be very careful if you go off in the woods to-day, looking for an adventure," said Miss Fuzzy Wuzzy.

"I will," promised the bunny rabbit gentleman.

Away he hopped on his red, white and blue striped rheumatism crutch, and his tall, silk hat. And this time Uncle Wiggily

44

took with him his glasses, which he sometimes wore in order to see better.

"And I want to see the very best I can to-day," said Mr. Longears to himself, as he hopped along. "I want to see that bad, unpleasant dog before he sees me!"

Uncle Wiggily was skipping along, thinking perhaps that he had better pick a bunch of violets and take them to the lady mouse teacher in the hollow stump school, when, all of a sudden, there sounded through the woods a loud:

"Wuff! Wuff!"

"That isn't the Fox, nor yet the Wolf, nor even the Skillery Scallery Alligator," said Uncle Wiggily, looking around the corner of the mulberry bush. "I think it must be that savage dog!"

And, surely enough it was. And a moment later the dog came bursting through the bushes, barking and growling and headed straight for Uncle Wiggily.

"I'll make believe I'm playing baseball and try for a home run!" said the rabbit gentleman to himself, and through the bushes, turning and twisting this way and that, he ran for his hollow stump bungalow.

Uncle Wiggily reached it only just in time, too. For as he hopped up the steps, and closed the door, locking it, the dog jumped over the gate.

"My goodness me sakes alive and a basket of soap bubbles!" cried Nurse Jane. "What's the matter, Wiggy? Is the house on fire?"

"It's that dog—chasing—me!" panted the bunny, for he was quite out of breath.

"The idea! How impolite of him!" exclaimed the muskrat lady, and she shook her broom out of the window at the bad chap.

"Well, you got away from me this time, but the next time I'll get you," growled the dog, as he slunk away.

"Why is he so anxious to catch you?" asked Nurse Jane, as Uncle Wiggily sat down in an easy chair to rest.

"Oh, I guess he'd chase any of the animal folk he saw in the wood," answered the bunny gentleman. "He'd chase Sammie or Susie Littletail the rabbits, Johnnie or Billie Bushytail the squirrels and I'm sure he would make Lulu, Alice and Jimmie Wibblewobble, the duck children, lose their feathers in trying to flutter away from him."

"It's too bad," said Nurse Jane. "You ought to speak to Old Percival, the Policeman Dog about this bad chap."

"I shall," said Uncle Wiggily. He did, too, but the bad dog was so sly that Old Percival could not catch him. Uncle Wiggily also spoke to the little dog, whom he had saved from having a tin can tied on his tail by a bad boy.

"I'll tell this savage dog to let you alone," the little chap promised.

But all this did no good. Every time the bad dog saw Uncle Wiggily in the woods he chased the rabbit gentleman, and once nearly caught the bunny. I don't know why this dog was so unpleasant and mean toward Uncle Wiggily. I guess maybe the dog didn't know any better. Perhaps he thought Uncle Wiggily didn't like dogs, but Mr. Longears did—especially Jackie and Peetie Bow Wow, the little puppy chaps.

Well, as it happened, one day the people who owned the big, savage dog, that always chased Uncle Wiggily, went away on a visit. And they went in such a hurry that they left the dog chained to his kennel, and they forgot to leave him any water to drink, or food to eat.

At first the dog was not hungry, but later in the day, when it was time for him to have had a meal, and some water, that dog began to feel very unhappy.

"Bow! Wow! Wow!" he barked, trying to call someone out to feed him, and pour water in the sun-dried pan. But no one came, and the dog grew more hungry, and so thirsty that his tongue hung down out of his mouth.

Just about this time Uncle Wiggily was going through the woods on his way to the six and seven cent store to get Nurse Jane a spool of thread. The bunny rabbit heard the barking of the dog, and started to run, for he knew that voice. But as he paused to listen, and find out from which direction the sound came, so he could run away from it, instead of toward it, Uncle Wiggily heard a voice saying:

"Bow wow! Oh, how hungry I am! How thirsty I am!"

It was the savage dog speaking, and Uncle Wiggily of course understood animal talk, even better than he had learned to know, as he had of late, what boys and girls said.

"Hum! So that dog is hungry and thirsty, is he?" said the bunny to himself. "Well, why doesn't he go and dig up some of the bones he must have buried? And why doesn't he go to the duck pond and get a drink, I wonder?"

Uncle Wiggily thought there was something strange about this, and as the barking and animal-talking voice of the dog did not come any nearer, the bunny hopped over to see what was the matter.

There he saw the savage dog, fastened by a heavy chain to his kennel, with nothing to eat, no water to drink and no one to bring him any.

"Oh, how hungry I am! How thirsty I am!" barked the dog.

"Oh, are you?" politely asked Uncle Wiggily

"Oh, are you?" politely asked Uncle Wiggily, looking out from behind a stone. He was not afraid to be this near the bad dog, for the savage chap was chained, and could not get loose.

"Yes, I am very thirsty and hungry," whined the dog. "But of course I don't expect you to feed me or give me water. I've been too bad to you—I've chased you too often! I can't ask you to help me!"

"I don't see why not," said Uncle Wiggily politely. "If I were ill in my bungalow, with rheumatism, and Nurse Jane wasn't there to wait on me, and you came along, wouldn't you get me a drink of water?"

The dog thought a moment before answering. Then he sort of drooped his tail, sorry-like and softly said:

"Yes, I believe I would."

"Then," said the bunny gentleman, "I'll bring you a drink, and if you tell me where you have buried some bones, I'll dig them up for you, since I can't loosen your kennel chain to let you dig them yourself."

"Oh, how kind you are!" said the dog. "I—I really don't deserve this."

"Stuff and nonsense!" laughed Uncle Wiggily. "We all make mistakes—that's why they put rubbers on the end of lead pencils, as someone has said. I'll help you when you're in trouble."

Then the bunny found a half a cocoanut shell, and dipping this in the nearby brook, brought water to the thirsty dog. And when he had taken a long drink, cooling his parched and hot tongue, the dog pointed to where he had buried some bones, behind the barn.

Uncle Wiggily dug up the bones with his paws, which were just made for such work, and carried them to the dog.

"Oh, I can't thank you enough," said Gurr-Rup, which was the dog's name. "And I promise, Mr. Longears, that I'll never chase you again."

"Thank you!" laughed the bunny, as he hopped on to the three and four cent store. "I hoped you wouldn't."

So this teaches us that it doesn't hurt the needle to put the thread in its eye, and if the apple doesn't jump out of the dumpling, and try to hide in the chocolate cake, when it ought to take the pie to the moving pictures, on the next page you will find a story about Uncle Wiggily and Puss in Boots.

STORY VIII

UNCLE WIGGILY AND PUSS IN BOOTS

"WHERE are you going, Uncle Wiggily?" called Nurse Jane Fuzzy one day, as the muskrat lady saw the bunny gentleman hopping away from his hollow stump bungalow.

"I am going to get myself a new pair of rubber boots," said Mr. Longears. "My old ones are wearing out, and they have little holes in, so they leak. We have had so much rain, of late, that I will need a new pair of boots if I am to look for any more adventures. So I am going to the shoemaker's."

"But why are you taking your old boots along?" asked Nurse Jane, for Uncle Wiggily had them under his paw.

"I am taking them to the shoemaker to show him what size I want my new boots," answered the bunny. "Also he may be able to mend these old ones so they will do to wear in the garden."

"That's a good idea," said Miss Fuzzy Wuzzy. "And while you are out I wish you would go to the seven and eight cent store for me. I want some needles and thread, some balls of red yarn and some white flannel."

"My! All that! Are you going to make a bedquilt?" asked the bunny gentleman.

"No," laughed Nurse Jane. "I am going to use the white flannel to make me a new petticoat, the red yarn I am going to use to knit Sammie and Susie Littletail, the rabbit children,

51

some mittens, and the needle and thread I will use to sew up a hole in the lace curtain."

"Very well," spoke Uncle Wiggily politely, "you shall have all three, and I'll get myself a new pair of boots."

It did not take the bunny rabbit gentleman long to hop to the shop of the Monkey Doodle shoemaker, where Mr. Long-ears bought himself a new pair of rubber boots.

"As for those old ones," said the Monkey chap, "I can mend them for you, so they will do to wear many times yet."

"Please do so," begged the bunny. And when his old boots were mended he carried them over his shoulder with the new ones, for he was wearing his shoes. Along he hopped to the seven and eight cent store.

Uncle Wiggily bought the needles, thread, white flannel and red yarn for the rabbit children's mittens, and he was hopping back to his hollow stump bungalow, when, all of a sudden, coming from behind a sassafras bush, he heard a voice saying:

"Oh, dear! How sad! Now I suppose they'll take me out of all the story books, and the children will never love me any more!"

"Hum! This is strange," said Uncle Wiggily to himself. "I wonder who it is that can't be in the story books any more? That is very sad! I wouldn't want them to put me out of all the Bedtime Story Books in which I have my adventures."

So the bunny gentleman looked around the corner of a lolly-pop bush, and there he saw a cat, dressed in a coat, trousers and cap, but without anything on his hind paws, sitting on a stump.

"Good afternoon, Mr. Cat!" politely greeted Uncle Wiggily. "You seem to be in trouble."

"I am," was the answer. "Only my name is Puss, and not Cat, though, of course, that's what I really am. Puss in Boots is my right name, but there is no use trying to keep it any longer."

"Why not?" Uncle Wiggily asked.

"Because I have lost my boots," answered Puss. "A little

"I have lost my boots," answered Puss

while ago I met a cross dog who chased me. I ran across a swamp and became stuck in the mud. I managed to pull my paws out of the boots, but the boots themselves remained fast in the mud. Now I have no boots and I can be called Puss in Boots no longer! I shall have to keep out of all the story books!"

"Nonsense!" laughed Uncle Wiggily. "Why, I have two pairs of boots here! Take one of them, I can only wear one pair of boots at a time," and very politely Mr. Longears gave his new boots to the cat.

"Oh, but I can't take your new boots!" objected Puss. "The old ones will do me very well."

"No," kindly insisted Uncle Wiggily. "Please take the new ones. Since my old ones were mended they will answer me very well, and they'll be easier on my paws."

So Uncle Wiggily gave Puss the new boots, keeping the old mended ones for himself, and as the cat put the boots on his paws he looked just as he ought to—like his pictures in the story books.

"Now I can keep my place, the children will not miss me. Thank you, Uncle Wiggily," mewed Puss.

"Pray do not mention it," said the bunny. "I am glad I don't have to carry two pairs of boots."

So Mr. Longears hopped on a little farther, and soon he heard some tiny voices saying:

"Oh, Mother dear! Look here! Look here!
Our mittens we have lost!"

"Ho! I should know who they are!" said the bunny. "Those must be the three kittens!"

And, surely enough, they were, as the bunny saw a moment later, when he turned around the corner of a mulberry tree. There were three little pussy kittens, holding up their paws for their mother to see, and there wasn't a single mitten on any one of the paws! What do you think of that?

"What, lost your mittens! You careless kittens!
Now you can't have any pie!"

Thus sang the mother cat. And when the three little kittens, who had lost their mittens, began to cry, Uncle Wiggily felt so sorry for them that he stepped up and said:

"Excuse me, Mrs. Cat. But I have a lot of red yarn I bought for Nurse Jane to knit mittens for Sammie and Susie Littletail. There is more than Miss Fuzzy Wuzzy needs, I'm sure, so I shall give you some to knit mittens for your pussies."

"Oh, how kind you are!" mewed the mother cat, as Uncle Wiggily gave her three balls of red yarn, still leaving plenty for the rabbit children's mittens. "Now you may have some pie, and I'll give Uncle Wiggily a piece, too," said the cat mother to her kittens.

"You are very kind," remarked Mr. Longears. "But I must hop on with the needle and thread, and the piece of white flannel Nurse Jane is going to use to make herself a new petticoat."

So on hopped the bunny, while the mother cat sat down to knit some new mittens for her kittens. And Uncle Wiggily had not gone very far before, all of a sudden, he heard another sad mewing sound and a voice said:

"Dear me! The hole goes all the way through! I shall never be able to go to see Old Mother Hubbard this way! Oh, what an accident!"

"That sounds like more trouble," thought Uncle Wiggily, and, looking over the top of a stone wall, he saw a pussy cat lady sitting on a stump, sadly looking at her skirt.

"What is the matter?" asked Mr. Longears.

"Oh! How you surprised me!" mewed the cat lady. "But here is the trouble. I'm Pussy Cat Mole. I jumped over a coal, and in my best petticoat burned a great hole!" and she showed the edge of her petticoat where, surely enough, a hole was burned through.

"And I ought to be at Mother Hubbard's now, to go with her to the movies," said Pussy Cat Mole. "But, alas, I can not go!"

"Oh, yes, you can!" said Uncle Wiggily.

"Not with this big burned hole in my petticoat!" mewed the cat.

"Ah, but you shall sew on a patch," said the bunny. "I have here needle and thread, and some white flannel. Can't you mend your best petticoat with all those?"

"Indeed I can," mewed Pussy Cat Mole. "Thank you, so much!"

Uncle Wiggily gave her a needle and thread, and with her claws Miss Mole tore off a piece of white flannel, for there was more than Nurse Jane needed. She sewed the patch neatly on, and then, with her petticoat nicely mended, Pussy Cat Mole went on to Mother Hubbard's.

"Ah, how delightful it is to be helpful," said Uncle Wiggily, as he hopped back to his bungalow. And he was very glad he had met the three cats, one after another. For a little later that day the bad Woozie Wolf chased the bunny.

But the mother of the three kittens, after she had knit their mittens, tickled the wolf with her knitting needles. Puss with the boots, stepped on the wolf's tail so hard that he cried "Ouch!" And Pussy Cat Mole ran at the wolf with a piece of red stone, which she pretended was a red hot coal that in her best petticoat had burned a great hole.

"I'll burn you! I'll burn you!" she mewed at the wolf.

"Then this is no place for me!" he howled, and away he ran, not hurting the bunny at all. And how the bunny gentleman and the three cats laughed!

So if the elephant from the Noah's Ark doesn't drop a cold penny down the back of the gold fish and make it sneeze, the next story is going to be about Uncle Wiggily and the lost boy.

STORY IX

UNCLE WIGGILY AND THE LOST BOY

"THERE goes that boy out again, flying his kite," said Nurse Jane Fuzzy Wuzzy, as she looked from the window of the hollow stump bungalow one morning.

"What boy?" Uncle Wiggily wanted to know.

"The new boy who has just moved into the red brick house," answered the muskrat lady housekeeper. "I hope he isn't a bad boy, who will chase you, Uncle Wiggily, and come to the forest to play tricks on Sammie and Susie Littletail, and the other animal boys and girls."

"Oh, he doesn't look like that kind of a boy," said the bunny rabbit gentleman, as he sat down to eat his breakfast of carrot pancakes with turnip maple sugar gravy sprinkled down the middle. "But I'll be careful until I get to know him better."

Uncle Wiggily's hollow stump bungalow had lately been rebuilt near the edge of a wood, and, just beyond the thicket of trees and tangle of bushes was a small town, where lived many boys and girls.

Only a few of these boys and girls knew about the bunny rabbit gentleman, and his muskrat lady nurse, and those who did were kind to Uncle Wiggily, because the rabbit gentleman had been kind to them, doing them many favors.

But now that a new boy had moved into the red brick house, Uncle Wiggily felt that he must not hop around in too lively a

58

fashion, until he found out whether the boy was bad or good. For there are some bad boys, you know.

"He seems quiet enough," said Nurse Jane, as she spread some lettuce marmalade on a slice of bread for Uncle Wiggily. "He sits there flying his kite. I guess it will be safe for you to go to the store for me, Wiggy."

"What do you want from the store?" asked the bunny gentleman, as he took his tall, silk hat down off the piano. Sometimes he went to the store quite dressed up. At other times he would put on an old cap and overalls, just as he came from the garden.

"I want another ball of red yarn," Nurse Jane answered. "I did not have quite enough to knit the mittens for Sammie and Susie, the rabbit children."

"I suppose that's because I gave some of the yarn to the three little kittens who lost their mittens," said the bunny, twinkling his pink nose upside down, to make sure it would not fall off as he hopped along.

"Well, that's one of the reasons," Nurse Jane answered. "But I'm glad you helped the little kittens. You can easily get me another ball of yarn."

"Of course," Uncle Wiggily agreed, and soon he was hopping over the fields and through the woods, on his way to the store. Not one of the stores where the boys and girls bought their toys and lollypops, but a special animal store, kept by a Monkey Doodle gentleman.

And as Uncle Wiggily hopped along under the bushes, near the house of the Kite Boy, the bunny heard the boy's mother say:

"Don't go away and get lost, Buddie!"

"No'm, I won't!" promised the boy, as he held his kite string in his hand and watched his toy fly high in the air.

Uncle Wiggily stopped for a moment, underneath a big burdock plant, and looked at Buddie, which was the boy's pet name. Buddie could not see the rabbit gentleman. If he had, Buddie would have been much surprised to notice a bunny with glasses and a tall silk hat.

The wind blew the kite higher into the air, and Uncle Wiggily thought of the many times he had helped Johnnie and Billie Bushytail, the squirrels, fly their kites, and how he had, more than once, made kites for Jackie and Peetie Bow Bow, the puppy dog boys.

Then the bunny gentleman hopped on to the store to get the ball of red yarn for Nurse Jane. He stayed some little time, Mr. Longears did, for he met Grandfather Goosey Gander, and talked to the old gentleman duck about rheumatism, and what to do when you sneezed too much.

But finally Uncle Wiggily started back for his hollow stump bungalow, and soon he was in the middle of the wood, about half way home. And all of a sudden the bunny gentleman heard a crying voice saying:

"Oh, dear! Oh, dear! I don't know where my home is! I'm lost! Oh, dear! I'm lost!"

Mr. Longears peered through the bushes, and there he saw the boy from the red brick house, who held in his hand a broken kite.

"Ah, I see what has happened!" said the bunny. "His kite broke loose from the string. Forgetting what he promised his mother, about not going away, the boy ran after his kite, over into the woods, and now he is lost. I wonder if I can help him find his way home?"

Uncle Wiggily did not show himself yet. Hiding behind the bushes, the bunny followed the lost boy as he wandered about among the trees, not knowing which way to go.

"Oh, where is my house?" said the boy over and over again. "Why can't I find it?"

Then a mournful voice cried:

"Woo! Woo! Woo!"

"Oh, dear! What's that?" exclaimed the lost boy, suddenly stopping.

"It's only an owl bird," said Uncle Wiggily to himself. He wished he might speak to the boy, and tell him this, but though the bunny could understand boy-talk, the boy couldn't understand rabbit language.

The Kite Boy went on a little farther, and then he heard a rustling in the dried leaves.

"Oh-o-o-o!" gasped the lost boy. "Maybe that's a snake!"

"Nonsense!" laughed Uncle Wiggily to himself. "It is only a brown thrush bird, scattering the leaves to look for something to eat. And, even if it were a snake it wouldn't hurt the boy. I wish I might tell him so."

The boy wandered along a little farther, and suddenly there boomed out through the forest a sound of:

"Ga-rump! Ga-roomp! Ga-Zing!"

"Oh, maybe that's a giant!" cried the boy, dropping his broken kite.

"Ha! Ha!" laughed Uncle Wiggily. "That's only Grandpa Croaker, the big bull frog who tells such funny stories to Bully and Bawly No-Tail, the frog boys! How Grandpa Croaker will laugh when I tell him the lost boy thought him a giant! But I must help this boy out of the woods, or his mother will be worried.

"Let me see, how can I do it without letting him see me? Ha! I have it. This ball of red yarn. I'll hop to the edge of the wood, near his house, and fasten one end of the red yarn to a tree there. Then I'll come back, unwinding the ball on the way, and when I get to the boy, I'll toss him what is left

It lead the boy home

of the ball. Then all he'll have to do will be to follow the red cord right to his house."

No sooner said than **done!** Uncle Wiggily knew his **way** through the forest, even in the dark, and he soon reached the edge of the wood and saw the boy's red brick house.

Then, tying one end of the red yarn to the bush near where the boy had been sitting to fly his kite, Uncle Wiggily turned back, unrolling the ball as he hopped along. He soon came to the lost boy again, and the poor little chap was crying harder than ever.

Over the bush and at the feet of the boy, the bunny tossed the little ball of yarn that remained.

"Oh, what's that?" cried Buddie, almost ready to jump out of his skin. But when he saw the little red ball, and the red string stretching off through the trees, he was no longer afraid.

"Oh, maybe this is a fairy string, and will lead me home!" he joyfully cried, as he began to follow it. And, though we know it wasn't a fairy string, still it was just as good, for it led the boy home, as he followed the yarn, winding up the ball as he walked along. And, oh, how fast he ran when he came within sight of his house, crying, as he dropped the ball:

"Here I am, Mother! Here I am. I'm not lost any more!"

"Well, I'm glad of that," Mother answered. "You shouldn't have gone into the woods. I was just coming to look for you."

"Well," whispered Uncle Wiggily to himself, "I'm glad I could be of some help in this world." Then the rabbit, who had followed the lost boy until Buddie found his home, wound up the red yarn again, and took it to Nurse Jane.

"My! That was quite an adventure," said the muskrat lady when the bunny gentleman told her about it. And if the boiled egg doesn't try to go sailing in the gravy boat, and splash condensed milk on the bread-knife, I'll tell you on the page after this about Uncle Wiggily and Stubby Toes.

STORY X

UNCLE WIGGILY AND STUBBY TOES

THERE are some children who are always stubbing their toes and falling down. That was what happened, far too often, to the little boy in this story. And I am going to tell you how Uncle Wiggily helped cure him.

Perhaps you may think it strange that an old rabbit gentleman, with a pink, twinkling nose and a tall, silk hat could cure a boy of stubbing his toes. But this only goes to show that you never can tell what is going to happen in this world.

So we shall start by saying that, once upon a time, there was a boy who slipped and stumbled so often that he was called "Stubby Toes."

Stubby Toes was not a very big boy. In fact, one of the reasons he stubbed his toe so often (first the big toe of one foot, and then the big toe of the other foot), the reason, I say, was because he was so small. He had not yet grown up so that he knew how to step over things that lay in his path, causing him to stumble.

Why, sometimes that boy would stumble over a pin on the sidewalk. And again I have known him to trip and almost fall because he saw, in his way, a leaf from a tree.

"Upsi-daisey!" his sister would cry as she caught him by the hand, so he would not fall. "Upsi-daisey, Stubby Toes!"

It was Sister who really gave Stubby Toes his name, but she was only in fun, of course.

Well, one day when Uncle Wiggily had started out of his hollow stump bungalow to look for an adventure, Sister took her little brother Stubby Toes for a walk. And, as it happened, the path taken by Sister and Stubby Toes stretched along through the woodland where the bunny gentleman lived.

"I think I'll go see Baby Bunty to-day," said Uncle Wiggily to himself, as he hopped along, twinkling his pink nose in the sunshine. "I have a little touch of the rheumatism, and Baby Bunty is so lively, always playing tag, or something like that in the way of games, that she'll make me spry, and chase the pain away."

But as the bunny gentleman came near the place where the little boy and his sister were walking, all of a sudden Stubby Toes tripped over a little stone, about as large as the end of your lollypop stick, and—down he almost fell!

"Upsi-daisey!" cried Sister as she pulled Brother to his feet. "Upsi-daisey!"

"Oh, ho! Boo hoo! I—I stubbed my toe!" cried the little boy.

"Of course you did!" said Sister, laughing.

I think I forgot to tell you that Stubby Toes often cried when he slipped this way. Yes, almost every time he cried, and Sister wished he wouldn't, and so did Mother.

"Boo hoo! Boo hoo!" the boy wailed. "I bunked myself!"

Sister laughed and recited this little verse, which is a good one to sing whenever anything happens. It is a verse I read once, many years ago.

"Oh, fie,
Do not cry,
If you stub your toe.
Say 'Oh!'
And let it go.
Be a man,
If you can,
And do not cry!"

After Sister had sung this for Brother, she wiped away his tears, which just started to trickle down his cheeks, and they walked on again.

"This is a good little girl," said Uncle Wiggily to himself, for, hidden in the bushes he had heard and seen all that went on. "I wish I could teach Stubby Toes not to stumble so much. I wonder how I can? I'll ask Baby Bunty about it."

So Uncle Wiggily hopped on to Baby Bunty's bungalow, and, meanwhile Brother and Sister walked through the woods.

Well, I wish you could have seen what happened to Stubby Toes! But, no! Perhaps, on second thought, it is better that you did not. But, oh! So many times as he almost fell!

He tripped over a little baby angle worm, who was crawling to the store to get a loaf of cake for his mother. And next Stubby Toes almost landed on his nose, because the shadow of a bird flitted across his path.

"Oh, Stubby Toes!" cried Sister, as she kept him from falling on his face. "Will you ever learn to walk without stumbling?"

"Boo hoo!" was all that Stubby Toes answered, for, just then he tripped over a blade of grass, and this time he fell down all the way. Only he happened to land on some soft, green moss, so he was not much hurt, I'm glad to say.

"This is too bad!" Uncle Wiggily said to himself, for he had heard and seen it all. "I must get Baby Bunty to teach this little chap how to walk more carefully."

It was not far to the home of Baby Bunty. That little rabbit girl was out skipping her rope in front of her house.

"Tag, Uncle Wiggily! You're it!" she cried, as soon as she saw the bunny gentleman.

"Tut! Tut! We have no time for a game now," said Mr. Longears. "I want you to come with me, Baby Bunty, and teach Stubby Toes a lesson," and he told about the little boy.

"Oh, I see what you mean," said Baby Bunty. "You want me to hop along in front of him, and show him how not to stub his toe."

"That's it!" said Uncle Wiggily. "Stubby Toes and Sister are kind to animals and will not harm us."

So, a little later, Uncle Wiggily and Baby Bunty were walking along the woodland path just ahead of the little boy and his sister.

"Now, Baby Bunty," said Mr. Longears, "show this boy how nicely you can hop along, even if there are sticks and stones on the path."

Away skipped the little rabbit girl. She came to a stone, but over it she stepped as nicely as you please. She reached a stick, but she gave a hop, and there she was on the other side! And she never stubbed her toe once, because she was careful!

By this time the little boy and his sister had seen Uncle Wiggily and Baby Bunty.

"Oh, look at the funny rabbits!" cried Stubby Toes. "I want to catch 'em!"

"No! No! Mustn't touch!" said Sister, and she reached out to catch hold of Stubby Toes, but it was too late! He tripped his foot on a dandelion blossom in the grass, and down he went!

"Boo-hoo!" he cried.

"Oh, fie!" said Sister, singing the little verse again. "Look at the baby rabbit! She doesn't stub her toes!"

And, surely enough, Baby Bunty, skipping along on the path in front of Stubby Toes, never fell once. She skipped over pebbles and stones, sticks and clumps of grass, and never once stepped on a flower.

"See if you can't do that, Stubby Toes!" begged Sister.

And of course that boy didn't want a little baby rabbit girl to walk better than he did. So he dried his tears, stood up straight and began to walk more firmly, watching where he set down his feet.

He came to a big stone and—over it he stepped without stumbling. He reached a stick—and, over that he put both feet without falling! He passed a lump of dirt—and right over it he JUMPED—and he didn't stub his toe once! What do you think of that?

"Oh, I'm not going to call you Stubby Toes any more!" laughed Sister. "Now you have learned to walk as well as that baby rabbit."

Uncle Wiggily laughed so hard that his tall silk hat almost slipped down over his pink, twinkling nose.

"I think we have done enough, Baby Bunty," he said, "Come on now, and I'll buy you a carrot lollypop!"

Away hopped the bunnies, and back home went Sister and Brother who was Stubby Toes no longer. Baby Bunty had taught him a good lesson.

And if the jumping jack doesn't fall off his stick when he is trying to play hop scotch with the bean bag, you shall next hear about Uncle Wiggily's Christmas.

STORY XI

UNCLE WIGGILY'S CHRISTMAS

Down swirled the snow, its white flakes blown by the cold December wind. From the North it came, this wind; and a bird—not a robin, for they had long ago flown South—a bird went in the barn, and hid his head under his wing, poor thing!

It was cold in the woods around Uncle Wiggily's hollow stump bungalow, and the rabbit gentleman brought in stick after stick of wood for Nurse Jane Fuzzy Wuzzy to pile on the blazing fire that roared up the chimney.

Uncle Wiggily, having filled the wood box, took his cap, and his fur-lined coat down from the rack.

"Dear me, Wiggy! You aren't going out on a day like this, are you?" asked Nurse Jane.

"Yes," answered the bunny gentleman, "I am, if you please, Nurse Jane. I promised Grandfather Goosey Gander I'd go down town shopping with him. He wants to look through the five and ten cent stores to see what they have for Christmas."

"Oh, well, if it's about Christmas, that's different," said the muskrat lady. "But wrap yourself up well, for it is storming hard. I don't want you to take cold."

"Nor do I want a cold," said Uncle Wiggily. "My pink nose gets very red when I sneeze. I'll be careful, Nurse Jane."

Out into the snowy, blowy woods went Uncle Wiggily. He passed the burrow-house where Sammie and Susie Littletail,

70

the rabbit children, lived. Susie was at the window and waved her paw to the bunny gentleman.

"Only three more days until Christmas! Aren't you glad, Uncle Wiggily?" called Susie.

"Indeed I am," answered Mr. Longears. "Very glad!"

Johnnie and Billie Bushytail, the squirrels, looked from the window of their house. Johnnie held up a string of nuts that he was getting ready to put on the Christmas tree.

"Billie and I are going to help Santa Claus!" chattered Johnnie.

"Good!" laughed Uncle Wiggily. "Santa Claus needs help!"

The bunny hopped along through the snow until he reached the kennel of Jackie and Peetie Bow Wow, the puppy dog boys.

"We're popping corn!" barked Jackie. "Getting ready for Christmas! That's why we can't be out!"

"Stay in the house and keep warm!" called Uncle Wiggily.

He hopped on a little farther until he met Mr. Gander, and the rabbit gentleman and the goose grandpa made their way through the five and ten, the three and four and the sixteen and seventeen cent stores. Each place was piled full of Christmas presents for animal boys and girls, and animal fathers and mothers were shopping about, to tell Santa Claus what to bring to the different houses, you know.

Uncle Wiggily saw some things he knew Nurse Jane would like, and Grandpa Goosey bought some presents that had come directly from the workshop of Santa Claus.

Then along came Mr. Whitewash, the Polar Bear gentleman.

"Ho! Ho!" roared Mr. Whitewash, in his jolly voice. "Come to my ice cave, gentlemen, and have a cup of hot, melted icicles!"

"I'd like to, but I can't," said Uncle Wiggily. "Nurse Jane wanted me to get her some spools of thread. I'll buy them and go back to my bungalow."

"Then I'll go with you, Mr. Whitewash," quacked Grandpa Goosey, and he waddled off with the bear gentleman, while Uncle Wiggily, having bought the thread, hopped toward his bungalow.

The bunny uncle had not gone very far before he heard some children talking behind a bush around which the snow was piled in a high drift. Uncle Wiggily could hide behind this drift and hear what was said.

"Is Santa Claus coming to your house?" asked one boy of another.

"I don't guess so," was the answer. "My father said our chimney was so full of black soot that Santa Claus couldn't get down. He'd look like a charcoal man if he did, I guess."

"It's the same way at our house," sighed the first boy. "Our chimney is all stopped up. I guess there'll be no Christmas presents this year."

"My! That's too bad!" thought Uncle Wiggily to himself. "There ought to be a Christmas for everyone, and a little thing like a soot-filled chimney ought not to stand in the way. All the animal children whom I know are going to get presents. I wish I could help these boys. And they probably have sisters, also, who will get nothing for Christmas. Too bad!"

Uncle Wiggily peered over the top of the snowbank. He

saw the boys, but they did not notice the rabbit, and Mr. Long-ears knew where the boys lived. Their homes were in houses near the brick one, where dwelt the lad who was once lost in the woods. Uncle Wiggily unwound a ball of red yarn, if you will kindly remember, and by following this the Kite Boy found his house.

"I wish I could help those boys who are not going to have any Christmas," said the bunny gentleman to himself, as he hopped on with Nurse Jane's spools of thread.

And just then, in the air overhead, he heard the sounds of: "Caw! Caw! Caw!"

"Crows!" exclaimed Uncle Wiggily. "My friends the black crows! They stay here all winter. Black crows—black—black—why, a chimney is black inside, just as a crow is black outside! I'm beginning to think of something! Yes, that's what I am!"

The rabbit's pink nose began twinkling very fast. It always did when he was thinking, and now it was sparkling almost like a star on a frosty night.

"Ha! I have it!" exclaimed Uncle Wiggily. "A crow can become no blacker inside a sooty chimney than outside! If Santa Claus can't go down a black chimney, why a crow can! I'll have these crows pretend to be St. Nicholas!"

No sooner thought of than done! Uncle Wiggily put his paws to his lips and sent out a shrill whistle, just as a policeman does when he wants the automobiles to stop turning somer-saults.

"Caw! Caw! Caw!" croaked the black crows high in the white, snowy air. "Uncle Wiggily is calling us," said the head crow. "Caw! Caw!"

Down they flew, perching on the bare limbs of trees in the wood not far from the bunny's hollow stump bungalow.

"How do you do, Crows!" greeted the rabbit. "I called you because I want you to take a few Christmas presents to some boys who, otherwise, will not get any. Their chimneys are choked with black soot!"

"Black soot will not bother us," said the largest crow of all. "We don't mind going down the blackest chimney in the world!"

"I thought you wouldn't," said Uncle Wiggily. "That's why I called you. Now, of course, I know that the kind of presents that Santa Claus will bring to the animal children will not all be such as real boys and girls would like. But still there are some which may do.

"I can get willow whistles, made by Grandpa Lightfoot, the old squirrel gentleman. I can get wooden puzzles gnawed from the aspen tree by Grandpa Whackum, the beaver. Grandpa Goosey Gander and I will gather the round, brown balls from the sycamore tree, and the boys can use them for marbles."

"Those will be very nice presents, indeed," cawed a middle-sized crow. "The boys ought to like them."

"And will you take the things down the black chimneys?" asked Uncle Wiggily. "I'll give you some of Nurse Jane's thread so you may easily carry the whistles, puzzles, wooden marbles and other presents."

"We'll take them down the chimneys!" cawed the crows. "It matters not to us how much black soot there is! It will not show on our black wings."

So among his friends Uncle Wiggily gathered up bundles

of woodland presents.   And in the dusk of Christmas eve the black crows fluttered silently in from the forest, gathered up in their claws the presents which the bunny had tied with thread, and away they flapped, not only to the houses of the two boys, but also to the homes of some girls, about whom Uncle Wiggily had heard.   Their chimneys, too, it seemed, were choked with soot.

But the crows could be made no blacker, not even if you dusted them with charcoal, so they did not in the least mind fluttering down the sooty chimneys.   And so softly did they make their way, that not a boy or girl heard them!   As silently and as quietly as Santa Claus himself went the crows!

All during Christmas eve they fluttered down the chimneys at the homes of poor boys and girls, helping St. Nicholas, until all the presents that Uncle Wiggily had gathered from his friends had been put in place.

Then, throughout Woodland, in the homes of Sammie and Susie Littletail the rabbits, of Johnnie and Billie Bushytail the squirrels, Jackie and Peetie Bow Wow the dogs, Curly and Floppy Twistytail the piggie boys—in all the homes of Woodland great changes took place.   Firefly lights began to glow on Christmas trees.   Mysterious bundles seemed to come from nowhere, and took their places under the trees, in stockings and on chairs or mantels.

And then night came, and all was still, and quiet and dark— as dark as the black crows or the soot in the chimneys.

But in the morning, when the stars had faded, and the moon was pale, the glorious sun came up and made the snow sparkle like ten million billion diamonds.

"Merry Christmas, Uncle Wiggily!" called Nurse Jane. "See what Santa Claus brought me."

"Merry Christmas, Nurse Jane!" answered the bunny. "And what a fine lot of presents St. Nicholas left for me! See them!"

"Oh, isn't he a great old chap!" laughed Nurse Jane, as she smelled a bottle of perfume.

And all over the land voices could be heard saying:

"Merry Christmas! Merry Christmas!"

Near the hearth in the homes of some boys and girls who had not gone to bed with happy thoughts of the morrow, were some delightful presents. How they opened their eyes and stared— these boys and girls who had expected no Christmas.

"Why! Why!" exclaimed one of the two lads whom Uncle Wiggily had heard talking near the snowbank. "How in the world did Santa Claus get down our black chimney?"

But, of course, they knew nothing of Uncle Wiggily and the crows. And please don't you tell them.

So all over, in the Land of Boys and Girls, as well as in the Snow Forest of the Animal Folk. there echoed the happy calls of:

"Merry Christmas! Merry Christmas!" Once again there was joy in the land.

And if the sunflower doesn't shine in the face of the clock, and make its hands go whizzing around backward, I shall take pleasure, next, in telling you about Uncle Wiggily's Fourth of July.

STORY XII

UNCLE WIGGILY'S FOURTH OF JULY

"You must be extra careful to-morrow, Uncle Wiggily," said Nurse Jane Fuzzy Wuzzy to the bunny rabbit gentleman one morning, as he stood on the steps of his hollow stump bungalow.

"Why be careful to-morrow, more than on any other day in the year?" asked Mr. Longears. "Is it going to rain or snow?"

"Whoever heard of snow on the Fourth of July?" inquired the muskrat lady housekeeper, as she fastened a fluffy brush to the end of her tail, for she was presently going in the house to dust the furniture.

"Oh, so to-morrow is the Fourth of July!" exclaimed the bunny. "I had forgotten all about it. Yes, indeed, I must be careful! I am living near the real children, now, and some of them might think it fun to explode a torpedo under my pink, twinkling nose, or try to fasten a fire-cracker to my little tail."

"That's what I was thinking of," went on Nurse Jane. For Uncle Wiggily's bungalow, while still in the woods, was near to the homes of some boys and girls. And though only one boy, so far, had been bad to the bunny (and this boy soon turned good), there was no telling what might happen.

So as Uncle Wiggily hopped along the forest path, he took care not to get too far away from the bushes, behind and under which he could hide. For sometimes boys and girls came to the

77

forest, and once a Kite Boy was lost, and the bunny helped him find his way home, you may remember.

"Hello, Uncle Wiggily!" suddenly called a voice, and Mr. Longears quickly jumped around, thinking it might be a real boy or girl. But it was only Neddie Stubtail, the little boy bear.

"I've been buying my fire-crackers," said Neddie to his uncle, the bunny. "I'm going to have lots of fun Fourth of July," and he showed Mr. Longears a bundle of dry sticks, painted red, white and blue like the bunny's rheumatism crutch.

You must know that in Animal Land the boys and girls have the same sort of fun you children do on holidays, but in a different manner. Instead of real fire-crackers, that have to be set off with a match, or piece of punk, with sparks that, perhaps, burn you, the animal children get some dried sticks. These they break, with loud, cracking sounds, but without any fire. And they have lots of fun. After the sticks are broken they can be put in the stove to boil the tea kettle.

"Did you get your sister, Beckie, any Fourth of July things?" asked Uncle Wiggily of the boy bear.

"Oh, yes, I got her some little stick crackers," answered Neddie.

"That's good!" spoke Mr. Longears. Then he went on through the woods, meeting Toddle and Noodle Flat Tail the beaver boys, Joie, Tommie and Kittie Kat the kittens, Nannie and Billie Wagtail the goats, and many other animal boys and girls. All of them called:

"Hello, Uncle Wiggily! Happy Fourth of July!"

And the bunny answered back:

"Thank you! I wish you the same!"

Thus hopping through the woods, meeting the animal children, and learning of the fun they were to have next day, the bunny rabbit gentleman at length came to the end of the forest. A little farther on were the houses and homes of real boys and girls, some of whom had been helped by Mr. Longears.

"I think this is as far as I had better go, seeing it's so close to the Fourth of July," thought Uncle Wiggily. "If the real children are anything like those of my animal friends who live in the woods, they'll be shooting off their crackers and torpedoes ahead of time."

And, just as he said that, Uncle Wiggily heard a loud: "Bang! Bung!"

The bunny jumped to one side, and hid under the broad leaf of a burdock plant. Then he laughed.

"I thought that was a hunter-man's gun," whispered Uncle Wiggily. "But I guess it was some boy setting off a fire-cracker. I need not have been afraid."

He was just going to hop along a little farther, before turning back to his hollow stump bungalow when, all at once he saw a hammock swinging between two trees near the edge of the wood.

In the hammock lay a boy with a thin, pale face, and beside him sat a nurse, gently pulling on a rope that caused the little nest-like swinging bed to sway to and fro.

"Oh ho!" thought Uncle Wiggily. "A sick boy! I'm sorry for him! He won't be able to run around and have fun on Fourth of July as Jackie and Peetie Bow Wow will."

And then the bunny heard the boy in the hammock speaking.

And, being able, as he was of late, to understand the talk of real persons, Uncle Wiggily heard the boy say:

"Do you think I'll ever be able to run around again, and have fun, and shoot off fire-crackers?"

"Of course you will," the nurse answered cheerfully.

"But I can't have any fire-crackers now, can I?" asked the boy, timidly, as though knowing what the answer would be.

"No, Buddie! You are not quite well enough," the nurse gently replied. "No fire-crackers for you!"

"How about torpedoes?"

"You couldn't have those, either, I'm afraid," and the nurse smiled as she leaned over to give the boy a drink of orange juice.

"Oh, dear!" sighed the boy in the hammock, just like that. "Oh, dear!"

Uncle Wiggily felt very sorry for him.

"I wish I could do something," thought the bunny gentleman. "This boy won't have much fun on the Fourth of July—not even as much fun as Curly and Floppy Twistytail, the piggie chaps, will have throwing corncobs against a tin pan and making believe they are skyrockets."

"Oh, dear!" again sighed the boy in the hammock. "Oh, dear!"

"What's the matter now?" asked his nurse.

"I don't s'pose I could even have a Roman candle, or a pinwheel, could I?" the invalid asked.

"Oh, indeed no!" laughed the nurse. "What a funny chap you are!"

But the boy didn't feel very funny.

Uncle Wiggily twinkled his pink nose. Then he put his tall, silk hat firmly on his head and, tucking under his paw his red, white and blue striped rheumatism crutch, off through the woods hopped the bunny uncle.

"I'm going to get some Fourth of July for that boy," said Mr. Longears. "He simply must have some."

Uncle Wiggily spent some time hopping here and there through the woods, and early the next morning, when the real boys and girls were shooting off real fire-crackers and torpedoes, and when the animal lads and lassies were cracking sticks and making torpedoes from broad, green leaves, Mr. Longears hopped to where the boy was, once more, swinging in his hammock.

The boy's head was turned to one side, and he was looking at some of his friends, over in the vacant lots, setting off fire-crackers. Uncle Wiggily, when the nurse wasn't looking, tossed into the hammock, from the bush behind which the bunny was hidden, a bundle of green things. They fell near the boy's hands.

Hardly knowing what he was doing the sick lad pinched one of the green things between his fingers.

"Pop!" it went.

"What's that?" cried the nurse. "It sounded like a fire-cracker."

The boy pinched another green leaf-like ball between his fingers.

"Pop!" sounded again, as the ball burst.

"Why," cried the nurse. "That's like a torpedo! What have you there, Buddie?"

"I don't know," the boy answered. "But these round, green balls, that burst and pop when I squeeze them, fell into my hammock. There's a lot of 'em! I can pinch them and make a noise for Fourth of July."

"So you can!" exclaimed the nurse, pinching one herself, and jumping when it went "Pop!"

"And they won't hurt me, will they?" asked the boy.

"No," answered the nurse, "they won't hurt you at all. They must have fallen off this tree, but I never knew, before, that such things as green fire-crackers grew on trees!"

"Ha! Ha!" laughed Uncle Wiggily to himself, hidden under a bush. "She doesn't know I brought the puff balls to the boy."

For that is what the bunny had done. In the woods he had found the green puff balls, inside which were the seeds of the plant. Later on, in the fall, the puff balls would be dry, and would crackle when you touched them, opening to scatter the seeds. But now, being green, and filled with air, they burst with a Fourth of July noise when squeezed.

'Oh, now I can have some fun!" laughed the sick boy, as he cracked one puff ball after another. "Hurrah! Now I'm celebrating Fourth of July!"

And he was. Uncle Wiggily had helped him, and the bunny gentleman had brought enough puff balls to last all day.

"Pop! Pop!" That is how they sounded as the boy pinched them in his hammock. Some were large, like big fire-crackers, and others were small, like little torpedoes.

"Oh, what a lovely Fourth of July!" sighed the boy, when

evening came to put the sun to bed, and the nurse wheeled the boy into the house.

And then, when it grew dark, Uncle Wiggily called together ten thousand firefly-lightning bugs, and they flittered and fluttered about the porch, on which the boy had been taken after supper. The fireflies made pinwheels of themselves, they went up like skyrockets, they leaped about in bunches like the balls from Roman candles and finally, when it was time to go to bed, they took hold of each others' legs and, clinging together, spelled out:

"Oh, it's just like real fireworks!"

"Oh, it's just like real fireworks!" cried the happy boy.

"I'm glad he liked it!" said Uncle Wiggily, as he hopped home to his hollow stump bungalow.

So if the pussy cat doesn't claw the tail off the letter Q and make it look like a big, round O, I'll tell you next about Uncle Wiggily and the little boy's skates.

STORY XIII

UNCLE WIGGILY AND THE SKATES

THERE was once a little boy to whom Santa Claus brought a pair of skates at Christmas. And, of course, that boy, as soon as he saw the shiny, steel runners, wished that the pond would freeze over so that he might try his new playthings.

"When do you s'pose there'll be skating?" he asked his mother again and again, for, as yet, there was only a "skim" of ice on the pond.

"Oh, pretty soon," his mother would answer. "You mustn't go skating when the ice is too thin, you know. If you did you would break through, into the cold water."

"And that would spoil my skates, wouldn't it?" asked the boy.

"Yes, but besides that you might be drowned, or catch cold and be very ill," Mother said. "So keep off the ice with your new skates until the pond has frozen good and thick."

"Yes'm, I will," promised the little boy, and, really, he meant to keep his word. But as the days passed, and the weather was not quite cold enough to freeze thick ice, the little boy became tired of waiting.

Every chance he had, after school, he would go down to the edge of the pond, and throw stones on the ice to see how thick it was. Often the stones would break through, and fall into the cold, black water with a "thump!" Then the boy would know the ice was not thick enough.

"I don't want to fall through like a stone," he would say, and back to his house he would go with his new skates dangling and jingling at his back, over which they were hung by a strap.

But one day, when the boy threw a large stone on the ice of the pond, instead of breaking through, the rock only made a dent and stayed there.

"Oh, hurray!" cried the boy. "I guess it's strong enough to hold me now! I'm going skating!"

However, first he started to walk on the edge of the ice near the shore, and when he did so, and heard cracking sounds, he jumped quickly back.

"I guess I'd better not try it yet," said the boy to himself. "I'll wait a little while until it freezes harder."

So he sat down by the edge of the pond to wait for the ice to freeze harder. But as he sat there, and saw how white and shiny it was, and as he looked at his new skates, which he had only put on in the house, that boy couldn't wait another minute.

He walked along the shore a little farther, to a place where the ice seemed more hard and shiny and there, after throwing some stones, and venturing out a little way, finding that there was no cracking sound, the little boy made up his mind to try to skate. There was no one else on the pond—no other boys and girls, and it was a bit lonesome. But the boy was so eager to try his new skates that he did not think of this.

Down he sat on the ground, and began putting on his Christmas skates. And it was just about this time that Nurse Jane Fuzzy Wuzzy, Uncle Wiggily's muskrat lady housekeeper, happened to look out of the window of the hollow stump bungalow. The bunny's bungalow was so hidden in the woods, near the pond, that few boys or girls ever saw the queer little house. But Uncle Wiggily could see them, as they came to the woods winter and summer, and often he was able to help them.

"Well, I declare!" exclaimed Nurse Jane, as she looked out of the window a second time.

"What's the matter?" asked Uncle Wiggily, who was just finishing his breakfast of lettuce bread and carrot coffee, with some turnip marmalade.

"Why, there's a boy—a real boy and not one of the animal chaps—getting ready to go skating!" said the muskrat lady, for she could see the boy putting on his skates.

"That ice isn't thick enough for real boys or girls to skate on," the bunny gentleman said. "It would be all right for Sammie Littletail, or Johnnie or Billie Bushytail, but real boys are too heavy—much heavier than my nephew Sammie the rabbit, or than the bushytail squirrel chaps."

"Well, this boy is going on all the same," cried Nurse Jane. "And I know he'll break through, and he'll frighten his mother into a conniption fit!"

"That will be too bad!" exclaimed Uncle Wiggily, as he wiped a little of the turnip marmalade off his whiskers, where it had fallen by mistake. "I must try to save him if he does fall in!"

"It would be better to keep him from going on the ice," spoke Nurse Jane. "Safety first, you know!"

"If I could speak boy language I'd hop down there and tell

him the ice is too thin," answered Uncle Wiggily. "But though I know what the boys and girls say, I cannot, myself, speak their talk. However, I think I know a way to save this boy, if he happens to break through the ice."

"Well, he's almost sure to break through," declared Miss Fuzzy Wuzzy, "so you'd better hurry."

"No sooner said than done!" exclaimed Uncle Wiggily, and, catching up his red, white and blue striped rheumatism crutch, and putting on his fur cap (for the day was cold), away the bunny hopped from his hollow stump bungalow.

Instead of going to the place where the boy, with his skates fastened on his shoes, was about to try the ice, the bunny gentleman went to the house of some friends of his. The house would seem queer to you, for all it looked like was a pile of sticks half buried in the frozen pond.

But in this house lived a family of beavers—queer animals whose fur is so warm and thick that they can swim in ice water and not feel chilly. In fact the beavers had to dive down under the ice and water to get into their winter home.

"Are Toodle and Noodle in the house?" asked Uncle Wiggily, as he reached the stick-house. On shore, not far from it, was Grandpa Whackum, the old beaver gentleman, with his broad, flat tail.

"Why, yes, Toodle and Noodle are inside," answered Grandpa Whackum. "Shall I call them out?"

"If you please," spoke Uncle Wiggily. "I want them to come and help me save a boy who, I think, is going to break through the thin ice with his new skates."

"That will be too bad!" exclaimed Grandpa Whackum.

Then with his broad tail he pounded or "whacked" on the ground, and soon up through a hole in the ice came swimming Toodle and Noodle Flat-Tail, the two beaver boys.

"Oh, hello, Uncle Wiggily!"

"Oh, hello, Uncle Wiggily!" they called. "We're glad to see you!"

"Hello!" answered the bunny gentleman. "Will you come with me, and help save a real boy?"

"Of course," said Toodle, shaking off some ice water from his fur coat.

"He won't try to catch us, will he?" asked Noodle.

"I think not," the bunny gentleman replied. "If what I think is going to happen, does really happen, that boy will be too surprised to catch anything but a cold! Come along, beaver chaps!"

So Toodle and Noodle, wet and glistening from having dived out of their house, and down under water to come up through the hole in the ice, followed Uncle Wiggily. The sun and wind soon dried their fur.

"There's the boy," said Uncle Wiggily, as he and the beaver chaps reached the edge of the pond. "He's skating on thin ice. He'll go through in a minute!"

And, surely enough, hardly had the bunny spoken than there was a cracking sound, the ice broke beneath the boy's feet and into the dark, cold water he fell.

"Oh! Oh!" cried the boy. "Help me, somebody! Oh! Oh!"

"Ha! It's a good thing Nurse Jane saw him!" said Uncle Wiggily. "Quick now, Toodle and Noodle! I brought you along because you have such good, sharp teeth—much sharper and better than mine are for gnawing down trees. I can gnaw off the bark, but you can nibble all the way through a tree and make it fall."

"Is that what you want us to do?" asked Toodle.

"Yes," answered Uncle Wiggily. "We'll go close to shore, where the boy has fallen in. Near him is a tree. You'll gnaw that so it will fall outward across the ice, and he can reach up, take hold of it and pull himself out of the hole."

By this time the poor boy was floundering around in the cold water. He tried to get hold of the edges of the ice around the hole through which he had fallen, but the ice broke in his hands.

"Help! Help!" he cried.

"We're going to help you," answered Uncle Wiggily, but, of course, he spoke animal language which the boy did not understand. But Toodle and Noodle understood, and quickly running to the edge of the shore they gnawed and gnawed and gnawed very extra fast at an overhanging tree until it began to bend and break. Uncle Wiggily gnawed a little, also, to help the beaver boys.

Then, just as the real boy was almost ready to sink down under water, the tree fell on the ice, some of its branches close enough so the boy skater could grasp them.

"Oh, now I can pull myself out!" he said. "This tree fell just in time! Now I'll be saved!"

He did not know that Uncle Wiggily and the beaver boys had gnawed the tree down, making it fall just in the right place at the right time. For the boy was so frightened at having broken through the ice, that he never noticed the bunny gentleman and the beaver boys on shore.

He caught hold of the tree branches in his cold fingers, pulled himself up out of the water, that boy did; and to shore. Then as he sat down, all wet and shivering, to take off his skates, so he could run home, Uncle Wiggily called to Toodle and Noodle:

"Come on, beaver boys! Our work is done! We have saved that boy, and I hope he never again tries to skate on thin ice."

Then Uncle Wiggily hopped toward his hollow stump bungalow, and the beaver boys slid on the ice, near shore, toward their own stick-house, for the pond was frozen hard and thick enough to hold them. And the boy ran home as fast as he could, and drank hot lemonade so he wouldn't catch cold.

He did get the snuffles, but of course that couldn't be helped, and it wasn't much for falling through the ice; was it?

"You never should have gone skating until the pond was better frozen," his mother said.

"I know it," the boy answered. "But wasn't it lucky that tree fell when it did?"

"Very lucky!" agreed his mother. And neither the boy nor his mother knew that it was Nurse Jane, Uncle Wiggily and the beaver boys who had caused the tree to topple over just in time.

But that's the way it sometimes is in this world. And if the cow doesn't tickle the man in the moon with her horns, when she jumps over the green cheese, I'll tell you next about Uncle Wiggily going coasting.

STORY XIV

UNCLE WIGGILY GOES COASTING

"Oh, it's stopped snowing! It's stopped snowing! Now we can go coasting; can't we, Mother?"

"And on our new Christmas sleds! Oh, what fun!"

A boy and a girl ran from the window, against which they had been pressing their noses, looking out to see when the white flakes would stop falling from the sky. Now the storm seemed to be over, leaving the ground covered with the sparkling snow crystals.

"Yes, you may go coasting a little while," said Mother. "But don't stay too late. When Daddy comes to supper you must be home."

"We will!" promised the boy and girl, and, laughing in glee, they ran to get on their boots, their mittens and warm coats.

"I want to go coasting! Take me to slide down hill!" cried Bumps, the little sister of the boy and girl. "I want a sleigh ride."

"Oh, Bumps, you're too little!" objected Sister.

"And she'll fall down and bang herself," added Brother. In fact the "littlest girl" did fall down so often that she was called "Bumps" as a pet name.

"I won't fall down!" Bumps promised. "I'll be good! Please take me coasting?"

93

"I think you might take her," said Mother.

"Yes, we will," spoke Sister. "Come on, Bumps!"

"Well, if she falls off the sled when it's going down hill, and she gets bumped, it won't be my fault!" declared Brother.

"I—I'll be good—I won't fall!" promised Bumps. So Mother bundled her up, and out she went to the coasting hill with Brother and Sister, each of whom had a sled.

"I'm not going to give her rides on my sled all the while!" said Brother, half grumbling.

"We'll take turns," more kindly suggested Sister. "Take hold of my hand, Bumps, and don't fall any more times than you can help, dear!"

"No; I won't," answered Bumps. The littlest girl was smiling and happy because she was going coasting with Sister and Brother. And she made up her mind she would try very, very hard not to fall.

On the other side of the forest, near which was the coasting hill of the children, lived Uncle Wiggily in his hollow stump bungalow. From afar he had often watched the boys and girls sliding down on their sleds, but the bunny gentleman had never gone very close.

"For," he said to himself, "they might, by accident, run over me. And, though I haven't much of a tail to be cut off, I would look queer if anything should happen to my long ears. I'll keep away from the coasting hill of the boys and girls."

But not far from the bunny's bungalow was another and smaller hill, down which the animal boys and girls coasted. Of course, very few of them had such sleds as you children have, with shiny steel runners, and with the tops painted red, blue, green and gold. In fact, some of the animal boys didn't bother with a sled at all.

Take Toodle and Noodle Flat-Tail, the beaver chaps, for instance. They just slid down hill on their broad, flat tails. And as for Johnnie and Billie Bushytail, the squirrels, they sat on their fuzzy tails and scooted down the hill of snow. Others of the animal children somtimes used pieces of wood, an old board or some sticks bound together with strands from a wild grapevine.

And about the time that Sister, Brother and Bumps went coasting, Sammie and Susie Littletail, the rabbits, passed the hollow stump bungalow of Uncle Wiggily Longears. The little bunnies were each pulling a sled made from pieces of birch bark they had gnawed from trees.

"Let's ask Uncle Wiggily to go coasting with us," spoke Susie.

"Oh, yes! Let's!" echoed Sammie. "It'll be lots of fun!"

And Uncle Wiggily was very glad to go coasting. Out of his bungalow he hopped, his pink nose twinkling twice as fast as the shiny star on top of the Christmas tree.

"Dear me, Wiggy!" cried Nurse Jane. "You don't mean to say you're going coasting with your rheumatism!"

"No, I'm going coasting with Sammie and Susie," the laughing bunny answered. "I haven't any rheumatism to go coasting with to-day, I'm glad to tell you." And, surely enough, he didn't need to take his red, white and blue striped crutch.

When Sammie, Susie and Uncle Wiggily reached the coasting hill, they found there many of the animal children.

"Oh, Uncle Wiggily! Ride on my sled!" invited one after another. "Ride on mine! Coast with me!"

"I'll take turns with each one!" promised the bunny gentleman, and so he did, riding with Sammie and Susie first, then with the Bushytail squirrel brothers, next with Lulu, Alice and Jimmie Wibblewobble, the ducks, and so on down to Dottie and Willie Flufftail, the lamb children.

Oh, such fun as Uncle Wiggily had on the animal children's coasting hill. And on the other side of the forest, Sister, Brother and Bumps had their fun, with the real boys and girls.

At last it began to grow dusk, and when Uncle Wiggily was thinking of telling the animal children it was time for them to leave for home, up came rushing Jackie and Peetie Bow Wow, the puppy dog boys.

"Oh, Uncle Wiggily!" barked Jackie. "We were just over to the big hill, where the real boys coast, and we saw——"

"We saw a little baby girl—that is, almost a baby—in a pile of snow!" finished Peetie, for his brother Jackie was out of breath and couldn't bark any more.

"What's that?" cried Uncle Wiggily. "A real, live little girl in the snow?"

"Right in a snow drift!" barked Jackie. "All alone!"

"Why," said the bunny gentleman, as he thought it over, "she must have been coasting with her brother or sister, and maybe she fell off a sled and went down deep in the snow. And they played so hard they never missed her! But she mustn't be allowed to stay asleep in the snow. She'll freeze!"

"If she's only a little one—almost a baby—couldn't we put her on one of our sleds?" asked Sammie.

"And ride her home," went on Susie.

"If we all pull together we'd be strong enough to pull a real, live girl, if she wasn't too large," quacked Jimmie Wibble-wobble, the duck.

"We'll try!" said Uncle Wiggily. "All of you take the grape-vine ropes from your sleds and follow me."

Quickly the animal children did this, taking with them only the large double sled of Neddie Stubtail, the boy bear, which was the largest sled of all. It was low and flat, and Uncle Wiggily thought it would be easy to roll a little girl up on it and pull her along.

Soon Uncle Wiggily and the animal children reached the hill where the real boys and girls had coasted. None of them was there now, all having gone home to their suppers.

"Here she is!" softly barked Jackie, leading the way to a snow bank, at the foot of the hill.

And there, sound asleep in the soft, warm snow was—Bumps!

Yes, as true as I'm telling you—Bumps!

The little girl had been sliding down with her sister, and had rolled off the sled at the bottom of the hill after about the forty-'leventh coast. And Bumps was so tired, and sleepy, from having been outdoors so long, that, as soon as she rolled from the sled into the snow, she fell asleep! Think of that!

And as Sister wanted to have a race with Brother and some of the other children, she never noticed what happened to Bumps. But there she was—in the snow asleep. Poor little Bumps!

"It will never do to leave her here!" whispered Uncle Wiggily to the animal boys and girls. "Don't awaken her, but roll her over on Neddie's sled, and we'll pull her to her home. I know where she lives. We'll leave her in front of the door, I'll throw a snowball to make a sound like a knock, and then we can run away. Her father and mother will come out and take her in."

So all working together, pushing, pulling, tugging and rolling most gently, the bunny gentleman and the animal boys and girls slid Bumps upon the low sled of the bear boy. Then they fastened the grapevine ropes to it, and, all taking hold, off they started over the snow toward the village.

It was almost dark, so no one saw the strange procession of Uncle Wiggily and his friends; and the bunny gentleman was glad of this. Right up to the home of Bumps they pulled her, and just as they got the sled in her yard Bumps opened her eyes.

"Oh! Oh! Oh!" she cried when she saw all the animal children, and Uncle Wiggily, too, standing around her. "I'm in fairyland! Oh, how I love it!"

"Quick, Sammie—Susie—Jackie—Peetie—scoot away!" called Uncle Wiggily in animal talk, and the rabbits, squirrels, guinea pigs, ducks, bears, beavers and others, all hopped away through the soft snow, out of sight. Uncle Wiggily tossed a snowball at the door, making a sound like a knock, and then the bunny gentleman also hopped away, laughing to himself.

He turned back in time to see the door open and Sister, Brother, Daddy and Mother rush out.

"Oh, here's Bumps, now!" cried Brother. "We must have forgotten and left her at the hill."

"Oh, that's what we did!" exclaimed Sister.

"Yes, but how did she get home?" asked Mother. "She never walked, I'm sure!"

"And look at the queer wooden sled!" said Sister.

"Who brought you home, Bumps?" asked Daddy.

"A—a nice bunny man, and some little bunnies, and squirrels, and a little bear boy and some ducks and chickens and little lambs and—and——" But Bumps was out of breath now.

"Oh, she's been asleep and *dreamed* this!" laughed Brother. "Some man must have found her and put her on this board for a sled, to bring her home."

"Nope!" declared Bumps, "it was a bunny! It was a funny bunny!"

"Bring her in the house!" laughed Mother. "She must have been dreaming!"

But we know it wasn't a dream; don't we? And if the strawberry shortcake doesn't go swimming with the gold fish in the lemonade and catch cold, I'll tell you next about Uncle Wiggily and the picnic.

STORY XV

UNCLE WIGGILY'S PICNIC

"Come on, Uncle Wiggily! Wake up! Wake up!" called Nurse Jane Fuzzy Wuzzy in the hollow stump bungalow one morning. "Come on!"

"What's that? What's the matter? Is the chimney on fire again?" asked the bunny gentleman, and he was so excited that he slid down the banister, instead of hopping along from step to step as he should have done.

"Of course the chimney isn't on fire!" laughed Miss Fuzzy Wuzzy. "But this is the day for the picnic of the animal children, and you promised to go with them to the woods."

"Oh, so I did!" exclaimed Uncle Wiggily, and he put one paw on his pink nose to stop the twinkling, which started as soon as he grew excited over thinking the chimney was on fire. "Well, I'm glad you called me, Nurse Jane. I'll get ready for the picnic at once. What are you going to put up for lunch?"

"Oh, some carrot bread, turnip cookies, lettuce sandwiches and nut cake," answered the muskrat lady.

"That sounds fine!" laughed Uncle Wiggily. "I'm very glad I'm going to the picnic!"

"Well, you had better hurry and get ready," remarked Miss Fuzzy Wuzzy. "Here come Jackie and Peetie Bow Wow to see if you aren't soon going to start."

100

Uncle Wiggily looked from the window of his hollow stump bungalow, and saw the two little puppy dog boys coming along.

Jackie was so excited that he stubbed his paw and fell down twice, while Peetie was so anxious to show Uncle Wiggily what was in the package of lunch the puppies were going to take to the woods, that Peetie fell down three times, and turned a back somersault.

"Uncle Wiggily! Uncle Wiggily! Aren't you coming?" barked Jackie.

"Hurry or it may rain and spoil the picnic," added Peetie.

"Oh, I hope not!" answered the bunny gentleman. "For if there is one thing, more than another, that spoils a picnic, it is rain! Snow isn't so bad. for we don't have picnics when it snows."

"Maybe it won't rain," hopefully spoke Nurse Jane, who was busy putting up lunch for Uncle Wiggily. "There isn't a cloud in the sky!"

And, surely enough, when Uncle Wiggily, Nurse Jane and dozens of animal children started off to the woods for their picnic, the sun shone bravely down from the blue sky and a more lovely day could not have been wished for.

The forest where the bunny gentleman, Nurse Jane and the animal children went for their picnic was a large one, with many trees and bushes. There were dozens of places for the squirrels, rabbits, goats, ducks, dogs, pussy cats and others to play; and when they reached the grove they put their lunches under bushes, on the soft cool, green moss and began to have fun.

"Oh, Uncle Wiggily! Please turn skipping rope for us?" begged Brighteyes, the little guinea pig girl.

"And please come play ball with us!" grunted Curly and Floppy Twistytail, the piggie boys.

"Have a game of marbles with us," teased Billie Wagtail, the goat, and Jacko Kinkytail, the monkey chap.

"I'll play with you all in turn," laughed the bunny gentleman. He was in the midst of having fun, and was just gnawing off a piece of wild grape vine to make a swing for Lulu and Alice Wibblewobble, the ducks, when up came hopping Bully No-Tail, the frog boy. Bully was quite excited.

"What's the matter, Bully?" asked Uncle Wiggily.

"Oh, gur-ump!" croaked Bully. "There is a big crowd of boys and girls over on the other side of the pond. They're having a picnic, too! Ger-ump! Ger-ump!"

"Real boys and girls!" added Bawly, who was Bully's brother. "Hump-bump!"

"Well, that will do no harm! laughed Uncle Wiggily. "Let the real boys and girls have their picnic. They will not see us, for very few boys and girls know how to use their eyes when they go to the woods. I have often hidden beside a bush close to where a boy passed, and he never saw me. Let the boys and girls have their picnic, and we'll have ours!"

So that's the way it was. Uncle Wiggily and the animal children played tag, and they slid down hill. Perhaps you think they could not do this in summer when there was no snow. But the hills in the forest were covered with long, smooth, brown pine needles, and these layers of needles were so slippery that it was easy to slide on them.

And then, all of a sudden, just about when it was time to eat lunch, it began to rain! Oh, how hard the drops pelted down! Rain! Rain! Rain!

"Scurry for shelter—all of you!" cried Nurse Jane. "Get out of the rain!"

The animal boys and girls knew how to take care of themselves in a rain storm, even if they had no umbrellas. Most of them had on fur or feathers which water does not harm. And they snuggled down under trees and bushes, finding shelter and dry spots so that, no matter how hard it poured, they did not get very wet.

They hid their lunches under rocks and overhanging trees so nothing was spoiled. And when the rain was over and the sun came out, as it did, the animal picnic went on as before, and when the food was set out on flat stumps for tables, there was enough for everyone, and plenty left over.

Nurse Jane was looking at what remained of the good things to eat when Jackie Bow Wow, who, with Peetie, had been splashing in a mud puddle, came running up wagging his tail.

"Oh, Uncle Wiggily!" barked Jackie. "What you think? Those real children, on the other side of the wood, they had their things to eat out on some stumps for tables, just as we had, and when the rain came, oh! it spoiled everything!"

"They didn't know how to keep their lunches dry," added Peetie. "Now they haven't anything to eat for their picnic, and they are starting home, and some of the little girls are crying."

"That's too bad!" murmured Uncle Wiggily, kindly. "Too bad that the rain had to spoil their picnic! Now we have plenty of things left that children could eat—nuts, apples, some pop-corn and pears," for the animal folk had brought all these, and many more, to the woods with them. "We have lots left over."

"We could give them something to eat," spoke Nurse Jane, "but how are we going to get it to them? We can't call them here; and it would never do to let them see us carrying the things to them."

"No," agreed Uncle Wiggily. "But I think I have a plan. We can make some baskets of birch bark. Some of the animal children—such as Jacko and Jumpo Kinkytail, the monkeys, Joie and Tommie Kat, Johnnie and Billie Bushytail, the squir-rels—are good tree climbers. Let them climb trees near where the real children are having their picnic, and lower to them, on grape-vine ropes, the food we have left."

"Oh, yes!" mewed Tommie, the kitten boy. "What jolly fun!"

Quickly Nurse Jane began to gather up the food. Uncle Wiggily put it in birch bark baskets the animal children made and then, with the baskets, fastened to vines, in their paws or claws, the animal boys went through the wood to the place of the other picnic. Uncle Wiggily and the remaining animal children followed.

There the poor, disappointed real children were, looking at their rain-soaked and spoiled lunches. Some of the little girls were crying.

"We might as well go home," grumbled a boy. "Our picnic is no good!"

"Mean old rain!" sighed a girl.

But just then the animal chaps with lunch from Uncle Wig-

gily's picnic—lunch which had not been rained on—climbed up
into trees over the heads of the boys and girls. Not a sound
did the animal chaps make. And when the real boys and girls
had their backs turned, there were lowered to the stump tables
enough good things for a jolly feast—apples, pears, popcorn,
nuts and many other dainties.

The animal boys scurried off

A little girl happened to turn around and see the birch bark
baskets of good things just as the animal boys scurried off
through the trees.

"Oh, look!" cried the girl. "The fairies have been here!
They have left us some lunch in place of ours that the rain
spoiled. Oh, see the fairy lunch!"

And I suppose that is as good a name for it as any, since the boys and girls didn't see Uncle Wiggily's friends lower the baskets from the trees. And the real boys and girls ate the lunch and had a most jolly time, and so did the bunny gentleman and his picnic crowd.

Now if the rubber plant doesn't stretch over and tickle the teapot so that it pours coffee instead of milk into the sugar bowl, you may next hear about Uncle Wiggily in the rain storm.

STORY XVI

UNCLE WIGGILY'S RAIN STORM

Down pelted the rain in Animal Land.

It also poured in Boy and Girl Land, which was on the other side of the forest from where Uncle Wiggily Longears lived in his hollow stump bungalow.

The bunny rabbit gentleman looked out of a window, and saw the drops fall drip, drip, dripping from trees and bushes, making little puddles amid the leaves where birds could come, later, and take a bath.

"You aren't thinking of going out in this storm; are you?" asked Nurse Jane Fuzzy Wuzzy, the muskrat lady bungalow-keeper, as she saw Mr. Longears putting on his coat.

"Why, I was, yes," slowly answered the bunny gentleman. "I am neither sugar nor salt, that I will melt in the rain. And, as it isn't freezing, I think I'll take a hop through the woods, and see Grandfather Goosey Gander."

"Well, as long as you are going out, I wish you'd go to the store for me," requested Miss Fuzzy Wuzzy.

"What do you want?" asked the bunny gentleman.

"Oh, bring a muskmelon for dinner," said Nurse Jane.

"A watermelon would be much easier to carry through the rain," Uncle Wiggily answered. "I think I'll bring a water-melon. If it gets wet no harm is done."

107

"All right," agreed Nurse Jane, laughing, so away hopped the bunny rabbit uncle, over the fields and through the woods. It seemed to rain harder and harder, but Uncle Wiggily did not mind. He had an umbrella, though he did not always carry one. It was made from a toadstool, and it kept off most of the rain. Though, as Mr. Longears said, he was neither a lollypop nor an ice-cream cone that would melt in a shower.

But not everyone was as happy as Uncle Wiggily in this storm. On the other side of the forest, as I told you, was Boy and Girl Land, and in one of the houses lived a brother and a sister. They, too, stood at the window, pressing their noses against the glass as the rain beat down, and they were not happy.

"Rain, rain, go away!
Come again some other day!
Brother and I want to go and play!"

That is the verse the little girl recited over and over again as she watched the rain pelting down. But the storm did not stop for all that she said the verse backward and frontward.

"Will it ever stop?" crossly cried the boy. "Why doesn't it stop?" and he drummed on the window sill, banged his feet on the floor and whistled. And his sister loudly recited over and over again:

"Rain, rain, go away!"

"Children! Children!" gently called Mother from where

she was lying down in the next room. "Can't you please be a little quiet? My head aches and I am trying to rest. The noise makes my pain worse."

"We're sorry, Mother," said the girl.

"But being quiet isn't any fun!" grumbled the boy. "Why can't we go out and play?"

"Because you would get all wet," answered his mother. "I've told you that two or three times, dear. Now please be quiet. It will stop raining sometime, and then you may go out."

"What can we play with?" asked the boy, not very politely I'm sorry to say.

"Why, some of your toys," replied his mother. "Surely you have enough."

"I'm tired of 'em!" grunted the boy.

"So'm I," echoed his sister.

Then she began once more to say the verse about the rain, as if that would do any good, and the boy rubbed his nose up and down the window, making queer marks.

Uncle Wiggily, on his way to see Grandpa Goosey Gander, and get a watermelon for Nurse Jane, took a short cut through a field, and passed the house where the children were kept in on account of the rain. And, as it happened, the window near which the boy and girl stood was open a little way at the top.

So, as the bunny gentleman hopped past, he not only saw the children, but he heard what they said, being able, as I have before related to you, to understand real talk.

But the children were looking up at the sky so intently, trying to see if it would stop raining, that they never noticed Uncle

Wiggily. Though if they had seen him, all dressed as he was like a gentleman from the moving pictures, they would have been very much surprised.

"Too bad those children have to stay in on account of the rain," thought Uncle Wiggily. "I wonder if I couldn't find some way of amusing them? If they are tired of their own playthings I might toss in, through the open window, some of the things the animal boys and girls play with. I'll do it!"

Off through the woods in the rain hopped Uncle Wiggily. He found a number of smooth, brown acorns, some of which had the cups, or caps still on. He filled one pocket with the acorns.

Next the bunny picked up some cones from the pine tree. There were large and small cones, and Nurse Jane always used one as a nutmeg grater, it was so rough, while Uncle Wiggily kept one near his bed to scratch his back at night.

"Let me see, what else would the animal children take?" said the bunny to himself. "I think they would take some green moss, and the girls would make beds with it for their dolls. The animal boys would take hollow reeds and blow little pebbles through them as real boys blow beans in their tin shooters. I'll take some moss and reeds."

This the bunny uncle did, also picking up some empty snail and periwinkle shells he found on the bank of a brook.

"The little girl can string these shells for beads," thought the bunny. "And I'll strip off some pieces of white birch bark so the boy can make a little canoe, as the Indians used to do."

Having gathered all these things—playthings which the animal children found in the woods every day—the bunny hopped back to the house of the boy and girl. The window was open, but the boy and girl had left it. The girl was giving her mother a drink of water, and the boy was bringing up some coal for the fire.

"This is my chance!" thought Uncle Wiggily.

Standing outside, he tossed in through the open window the acorns, the pine cones, the shells, the moss and other things. Then he hopped quickly away and hid behind a bush. He could hear the children come back into the room, and soon he heard the girl cry:

"Oh, look what the wind blew in! Some acorns! I can make little cups of them, and use the tops for saucers! And I'll set a play-party table for my doll, and decorate it with green moss. Oh, how perfectly lovely!"

"I'm going to make a boat out of this birch bark!" cried the boy. "And look! A hollow reed, like a bean blower! Now I can have some fun!"

"Look at the lovely shells I can string and make a necklace of!" went on the girl.

"And I can make wooden legs, and a wooden head and stick em on these pine cones and make believe they're Noah's ark animals!" laughed the boy. "Hurray!" he cried most happily.

"What is going on out there?" called Mother from where she was lying down. "Have you found something to play with?"

"Yes'm," answered the boy. "We'll be quiet now."

"And we don't care if it does rain," said the girl. "The wind blew a lot of lovely things in the window!"

But of course we know that Uncle Wiggily tossed them in.

"I guess they'll be all right now, no matter how much it

rains," said the bunny, as he hopped along to see Grandpa Goosey, and buy the snowmelon—excuse me, I mean the watermelon—for Nurse Jane.

So this teaches us that sometimes a rain storm is good for letting you find out new ways of having fun. And if the looking-glass doesn't make funny faces at the rag doll, when she's trying to see if her hair ribbon is on backward, on the next page you may read about Uncle Wiggily and the mumps.

NOTE

Uncle Wiggily specially requests that the following story will NOT be read to children who have the mumps. Please wait until they are better.

STORY XVII

UNCLE WIGGILY AND THE MUMPS

UNCLE WIGGILY LONGEARS, the bunny rabbit gentleman, was hopping through the woods one day, and he was thinking of making his way over to the other side of the forest, where the real boys and girls lived, hoping he might have an adventure, when, all at once, Mr. Longears heard some voices talking behind a mulberry bush.

"I know what we can do," said the voice of a boy, as Uncle Wiggily could tell, for he had learned to know the talk of boys and girls.

"What can we do?" asked the voice of another boy.

"We can pick up a lot of stones," went on the first boy, "and we can make believe we're hunters, and we can walk through the woods and throw stones at the birds, and squirrels, and rabbits! Come on! Let's do it!"

"Oh, no! I don't want to do *that*," said the second boy. "It isn't any fun to throw stones at birds and bunnies. If you hit a mother bird, and break her wing, she can't take anything to eat to the little birds, and they'll starve."

"Pooh! That's nothing!" exclaimed the first boy, and Uncle Wiggily peeked over the top of the bush to see what manner of boys these were. But the bunny rabbit gentleman kept himself well hidden.

"I don't want any stones thrown at me," he thought.

"And," went on the second boy, who seemed rather kind, "if you throw a stone at a rabbit you might break its leg, and then it couldn't hop home to the baby rabbits."

"That is very true!" thought Uncle Wiggily, who was listening to all that went on. "I wish there were more boys like this kind one."

"Well, I don't care!" grumbled the first boy. "I'm going off and throw stones at birds and rabbits and squirrels!"

"And I'm going home," said the second boy. "I don't feel very good. I have a pain in my cheek and maybe I'm going to have the toothache."

"Goodness me, sakes alive! I hope nothing like *that* happens to such a kind boy," thought Uncle Wiggily. "And as for that other chap, I'll run ahead of him, through the woods, and tell my friends to hide so he can't throw stones at them."

So, while one boy went home and the other picked up some stones, Uncle Wiggily skipped along through the woods, calling, in his animal talk, to his friends to hide themselves.

"For a boy is coming to stone you!" exclaimed the bunny rabbit gentleman. "Hide! Hide away from the stone-throwing boy!"

And so it happened that when the unkind chap came tramping through the woods, the only bird he saw to stone was an old black crow, as black as black could be.

"I'll hit you!" cried the boy, as he threw a stone.

But the crow was a wise old bird, and wasn't even afraid of the scary, stuffed men that farmers put in their cornfields. So the crow dodged the stone and then he laughed at the boy.

"Haw! Haw! Haw!" laughed the old black crow. "Haw! Haw! Haw!"

The boy grew very cross at this, and threw more stones, and some fell among the flower bushes where some bees were gathering the sweet juices of flowers to make into honey. One stone knocked a bee off a blossom, and spilled the honey it was gathering.

"Just for that I'm going to sting that boy!" buzzed the bee. Out it flittered, making such a zipping sound around that boy's head as to cause the bad chap to drop his stones and run away. So the bee did not have to sting him after all.

"Boys are no good!" buzzed the bee to Uncle Wiggily, as the honey chap flew back to the flowers.

"Oh, *some* boys are good," said the bunny gentleman. "The boy who was with this bad chap was good, and kind to animals. And that reminds me; this boy said he didn't feel very well. I must hop over to-morrow, and take a look at his house. I know where he lives. I hope he isn't going to have the toothache."

But the kind boy, as I call him just for fun, you know, had something worse than the toothache. His neck and jaws began to swell in the night, and he could hardly swallow a drink of water which his mother gave him when she heard him tossing in bed.

"What you s'pose is the matter of me, Mother?" asked the boy.

"Well," said Mother, as she smoothed his pillow, "perhaps you caught cold in the woods to-day."

But it was worse than that. When the Doctor came in the morning, and looked at the boy, and gently felt of his neck (even which gentle touch made the boy want to cry) the Doctor said:

"Hum! Mumps!"

"Did you say 'bumps,' Doctor?" asked the boy's mother. "Did he fall down and bump himself?"

"No, I said *mumps!*" exclaimed the doctor. "That's a swelling inside his neck, and it will hurt him a lot. But if you keep him in bed, and warm, and give him easy things to eat, he'll soon be all right again."

"Poor boy!" murmured Mother. "Well, I suppose *mumps* are better than *bumps*."

"I'm not so sure about that," spoke the Doctor as he walked to the door with the boy's mother. "Whatever you do," he said in a whisper, "don't give him anything *sour*—such as lemons or pickles. Sour things make the mumps pain more than ever. Don't even *speak* of vinegar in front of him, or so much as *whisper* it!"

"I won't," promised Mother.

But the boy's little sister overheard what Doctor and Mother were saying, and, being a mischievous sort of girl, she decided to have some fun. At least *she* called it fun.

"I'm going to stand in front of Brother and hold up a pickle so he can see it," said Sister to herself. "I want to see what he'll do!"

So Sister hurried down to the kitchen and brought up a pickle.

Then she went in the room where Brother was in bed and, holding the sour pickle in front of him, called:

"Look!"

And, no sooner did the boy look than he felt a sharp pain in his throat, almost as bad as toothache, and he cried:

"Go on away!   Stop showing me that—that——" Well, he couldn't even say the word "pickle," for just the thought of anything sour hurts your mumps, you know.

The boy hid his face in his pillow, and when he couldn't see the pickle he felt a little better.   But his Sister was still full of mischief.

"Lemons!   Lemons!   Nice sour lemons!" she called teasingly.

"Stop it   Stop it!" begged the boy.   "Oh, how my mumps hurt!   Mother, make Sister stop hurting my mumps!"

And when Mother came, and found what Sister was doing, she made the little girl go to bed, even though it was daytime.

"You will, very likely, get the mumps yourself," said Mother. "And I hope no one says anything sour to *you.*"

And, later on, Sister did get the mumps, but I'm glad to say her brother did not hold a lemon up in front of her.   For, as I told you, even the *thought* of anything sour hurts the mumps.

Now you know the reason why I didn't want you to read this story when you had the swelling in your neck.   It was better to wait until your mumps were gone; wasn't it?

So this boy had the mumps, and he had them on both sides at once, which is the very worst form.   He could hardly swallow anything because of the pain, even things that were not sour. Now and then he managed to sip a little hot chocolate.

His mother put a warm flannel bandage around his face, which was much swelled, and, thus wrapped up, the little boy could, now and then, get out of bed.

It was on one of these times, when his jaws were wrapped up, and his face swollen, that Uncle Wiggily happened to hop along through the woods, not far from the Mump Boy's house. And, having very good eyes, Mr. Longears saw the sick lad.

"Poor fellow!" thought the bunny gentleman. "He is ill, just as he thought he was going to be! Toothache it is, too!"

"Who has the toothache!" asked Dr. Possum, for the animal doctor came along just then, with his bag of medicine held fast in the curl of his tail.

"That boy," answered Uncle Wiggily, pointing from the bush, where he and Dr. Possum were hiding, to the window of the boy's home.

"He hasn't the toothache! Those are the mumps!" said Dr. Possum, who knew all about such things.

"Mumps!" exclaimed Uncle Wiggily. "Oh, that's too bad. Why, if that boy is mumpy he must have trouble eating. I wonder if I could leave on his doorstep something he would like— something that he wouldn't have to chew and which would slip down easily?"

"Whatever you leave for him, don't have it *sour*," advised Dr. Possum, as he hurried along to see Curly Twistytail, the piggie boy, who had cut his nose on a piece of glass while digging for wild sunflower roots in the woods.

"Ha! Nothing sour for the Mump Boy!" said Uncle Wiggily to himself, as Dr. Possum hopped away. "Then something sweet will be just the proper thing. Sweet honey! I have it!

I'll ask my friends, the bees, for some of their honey. I'll get Nurse Jane to make a little pail of birch bark, and I'll leave the wild honey on the boy's stoop."

Off hopped the bunny gentleman, until he found where the bees had their home in a hollow tree.

"Could you give me some honey for a good boy with bad mumps?" asked the rabbit.

"Some honey for a good boy with the bad mumps?" said the Queen Bee. "Certainly, Uncle Wiggily! As much as you like!"

Nurse Jane Fuzzy Wuzzy, the bunny's muskrat lady house-keeper, made a little box of white bark from the birch tree, and when this pretty box was filled with wild, sweet honey, Uncle Wiggily took it with him one evening.

It was time for the Mump Boy to go to bed, but the pain in his neck was so bad that he cried.

"I'm hungry, too," he said. "Oh, why can't I eat something that won't hurt my mumps?"

"I'll try to think of something for you," said Mother wearily.

Just then Uncle Wiggily hopped to the edge of the forest, close to the Mump Boy's house, and running up, he put the birch box of wild honey on the stoop. Then the bunny threw some little stones at the door and hopped away, hiding in the bushes.

"Wait until I see who's at the door," said Mother, as she smoothed the boy's pillow. "Then I'll get you something."

She looked out on the porch, and saw the little birch bark box.

"It looks like a valentine," she thought, "though this isn't Valentine's Day."

"What is it?" asked the boy. "Is it anything I can eat that won't hurt my mumps?"

"Why, yes, it is!" joyfully said his mother, as she saw what it was. "Sweet, wild honey!"

Even the name, so different from sour pickles or lemons, made the Mumps Boy feel better.

"Please give me some," he begged. "It sounds good!"

Uncle Wiggily
saw him
at the window

The wild sweet honey slipped down as gently as a feather, not hurting the boy's neck at all. And soon after that he went to sleep and in a few days he was better.

Uncle Wiggily saw the boy at the window, the bandage no longer on his face, and he even saw the boy eating the last of the wild honey.

"I guess he liked it," thought the bunny, as he hopped away.

When the boy was all better, and could be out and play, he asked all of his friends which one it was who had left the honey on the porch.   One and all answered:

"I didn't do it!"

"I wonder who it was?" said the boy, over and over again.

Well, we know; don't we?   But we aren't allowed to tell. And when the Boy's Sister caught the mumps, Uncle Wiggily left her some honey also.   Which was very kind of him, I think.

So if the little pussy cat doesn't drop her penny in the snow-bank, thinking it will turn into a dollar so she can buy a box of lollypops, you may next hear about Uncle Wiggily and the measles.

STORY XVIII

UNCLE WIGGILY AND THE MEASLES

ONCE upon a time there was a boy who didn't like to go to school. Every chance he had he stayed at home instead of going to his classes to learn his lessons.

Sometimes he would get up in the morning and say:

"Mother, I think I'm going to have the toothache. I guess I better not go to school to-day."

But his mother would laugh and say:

"Oh, run along! If you get the toothache in school the teacher will let you come home."

Then the boy would go to school, though he didn't want to, and he would be thinking up some new excuse for staying home, so really he did not recite his lessons as well as he might.

One day this boy came running in the house, all excited, and called out:

"Oh, Mother! I just know I can't go to school to-morrow!"

"Why not?" asked Mother.

" 'Cause I've been playing with the boy across the street, an' he's got the measles, an' I'll catch 'em an' I can't go to school. You ought t' see! He's all covered with red spots!" The boy who didn't like school was much excited. "He's all red spots!" he exclaimed.

"Is he?" asked Mother. "Well, the measles aren't painful, though they are 'catching,' as you children say. However, you

122

can't catch them quite as soon as one day. So you may go to school until you break out with red spots. Then it will be time enough to stay at home."

"Can't I stay home to-morrow?" begged the boy.

"Oh, of course not!" laughed Mother. "I want you to go to school and become a smart man! Time enough to stay home when you get the measles!"

Now, of course, this did not suit that boy at all. When he went to bed he was thinking and thinking of some plan by which he could stay home from school. For there was to be a hard lesson next day, and, though I am sorry to say it, that boy was too lazy to study as he ought.

"If I could only break out with the measles I could stay home," he kept saying over and over again as he lay in bed. Every now and then he would get up, turn on the electric light in his room and look at himself in the glass to see if any red spots were coming. But he could see none.

"What's the matter, Boysie?" his mother called to him from her room. "Why are you so restless?"

"Maybe I'm getting the measles," he hopefully answered.

"Nonsense! Go to sleep!" laughed Daddy.

Finally the boy did go to sleep, but either he dreamed it, or the idea came to him in the night, for, early in the morning, he awakened and, slipping on his bath robe. went into his sister's room.

"Hey, Sis!" he whispered. "Where's your box of paints?"

"What you want 'em for?" asked Sister.

"Oh, I—I'm going to paint something," mumbled the boy. Sister was too sleepy—for it was only early morning as yet—to wonder much about it, so she told her brother where to find the paints, and then she turned over and went to sleep again.

Now what do you suppose that boy did?

Why, he went back to his room, and with his sister's brush and color box he painted red spots on his face, just as he had seen them on the face of the real Measles Boy across the street. Then this boy put the paints away and waited.

After a while Mother called:

"Come, Boysie! Time to get up and go to school!"

"I—I don't guess I'd better go to school this morning," said the boy, trying to make his voice sound weak and ill and faint-like.

"Not go to school! Why not?" cried Mother in surprise.

"I—I'm all red spots," the boy answered. And when his mother went in his room, and saw that he really was spotted, she exclaimed:

"Why, you *have* the measles! I didn't think they'd break out so *soon!* Well, you must stay in the dark on account of your eyes. I'll bring you in some breakfast, and of course you can't go to school!"

Then that boy had to put the bedquilt over his mouth so he wouldn't laugh. If his room had been light his mother, of course, would have seen that the spots were only red paint. But in the dimness of early morning she didn't see.

"Isn't Brother going to school?" asked Sister as she ate her breakfast.

"He has the measles," said Mother. "I expect you'll come down with them next, and break out in a day or so. But wait until you do."

And if Sister thought anything about her red paint she said nothing. I don't believe she ever imagined her brother would play such a trick.

At first, after his sister had gone to school, and he had been given his breakfast in bed, the boy thought it was going to be lots of fun to pretend to have the measles and stay home from school. But after a while this began to grow tiresome.

It was a beautiful, warm sunshiny day outside, and staying in a dark room wasn't as much fun as that boy had thought. He could hear the bees humming outside his open window, and the birds were singing.

His mother opened the door and spoke to him.

"I'm just going across the street a few minutes," she said. "You'll be all right, won't you?"

"Yes'm," answered the boy. "My measles don't hurt hardly any."

And of course they couldn't, being only painted measles, you know.

When Mother went away, softly closing the door after her, the sound of the buzzing bees and the singing birds came to the boy through his window. He knew it must be lovely outside, and yet he had to stay in bed.

"But I can get up and run out for a little while," he said to himself. "Mother will never know!"

No sooner thought of than done! The boy quickly put on some clothes—not many, for it was summer—and out into the yard he went, his face all red paint spots. He didn't dare wash them off or his mother would have noticed.

Now it happened that Uncle Wiggily, the bunny rabbit gen-

tleman, was out that day, taking a walk with Grandfather
Goosey Gander. The two friends passed through the woods,
close to the edge of the yard of the house where the make-believe
Measles Boy lived. And the boy saw the bunny gentleman, all
dressed up as Uncle Wiggily was. Grandpa Goosey, also, had

"Hop faster!"
quacked Grandpa

on his coat and trousers. Uncle Wiggily wore his golf suit that
day—black and white checkered trousers and a cap.

"Oh, what a funny rabbit! What a funny goose!" cried the
boy. "I'm going to catch 'em and have a play circus in my
yard!"

Forgetting that he was supposed to be suffering from measles,
this boy chased after Uncle Wiggily and Grandpa Goosey.

"We'd better run," quacked the goose gentleman. "Boy, you know! Chase us! Throw stones, you know. Better run; what?"

"I believe you!" answered Uncle Wiggily. "Run it is!"

Off hopped the bunny! Off waddled the goose! But the boy was a fast runner, in spite of the red spots on his face and he came nearer and nearer to Uncle Wiggily.

"I'm afraid he's going to catch me, Grandpa!" spoke Mr. Longears in animal talk, of course, which the boy could not hear, much less understand.

"Hop faster!" quacked Grandpa, who was half running and half flying.

On came the boy! Grandpa Goosey, who was ahead, looked back and saw that Uncle Wiggily was soon going to be caught.

"There is only one way to save the bunny," thought Grandpa Goosey. "I'll splash some water in that boy's face and eyes so he can't see for a moment. Then Uncle Wiggily and I can get away!"

Near the path along which the boy was chasing the bunny and goose was a puddle of water. As quick as a wink Grandpa Goosey splashed into this, and, with his wings and webbed feet, he sent such a shower of water into the face of the boy that the bad chap had to stop.

"Oh! Ouch! Stop splashing me!" cried the boy. His face was all wet, but he wiped it off on his sleeve, and with his handkerchief. And when he had cleared his eyes of water he started to run again.

But by this time Uncle Wiggily and Grandpa Goosey were far off, hidden in the forest. and the boy could not find them.

"I guess I'd better go back home and get into bed," thought the boy. "Mother will be looking for me."

He was just going in the house when his mother came up the steps.

"Why, Boysie!" exclaimed Mother. "You shouldn't have gone out with the measles! Why—where *are* your measles?" she asked, for the spots were gone. "Your face is all red, like a lobster; but you haven't any more measles spots! What happened?"

The boy remembered the water that Grandpa Goosey had splashed up from the puddle. He took out his handkerchief and looked at it. That, too, was red!

"Why, it's *red paint!*" cried Mother. "Oh, Boysie! How could you play such a trick?" and she felt so sad that tears came into her eyes. "What made you do it, Boysie?"

"I—I didn't want to go to school," the boy answered, softly and much ashamed.

"Oh, how foolish of you!" said Mother. "Now I'll have to take you to school myself, but I won't tell teacher what you did—that is, I will not if you study your lessons well."

"I will, Mother! I will!" the make-believe Measles Boy promised. "I'll never want to stay home from school again!"

And he never did—even when he really had the measles which broke out on him about a week later. But he did not have them very hard, though he didn't need any of his sister's paints to make red spots.

And when Grandpa Goosey looked in the window of the boy's house, and saw the little chap with his face all speckled, the goose gentleman said:

"Serves him right for chasing Uncle Wiggily and me!"

Well, perhaps it did. Who knows? Anyhow, if it should happen that the doorknob doesn't turn around and try to crawl through the keyhole when the milk bottle chases the pussy cat off the back stoop, then I may tell you next about Uncle Wiggily and the chicken-pox.

STORY XIX

UNCLE WIGGILY AND THE CHICKEN-POX

ONE day Charlie and Arabella Chick, the little rooster and hen children of Mrs. Cluck-Cluck, the hen lady, came fluttering over to Uncle Wiggily's hollow stump bungalow.

"Oh, Uncle Wiggily!" cackled Arabella. "What you think has happened?"

"Well, I hardly am able to guess," answered the bunny gentleman. "I do hope, though, that your coop isn't on fire. You seem much excited, my dears!"

"Well, I guess you'd be excited, too, if a boy threw stones at you!" crowed Charlie. "Wouldn't you?"

"Indeed I would," admitted Uncle Wiggily. "Once a boy did stone me and I didn't like it at all."

"We don't like it either," cawed Arabella.

"Isn't there some way you can stop that boy from throwing sticks and stones at us?" Charlie wanted to know.

"Tell me about it," suggested Uncle Wiggily.

"Well, it's this way," began Arabella. "This boy lives on the other side of the Big Forest. Sometimes Charlie and I go over there to pick up beechnuts and other good things to eat, and every time that boy sees us he pegs things at us! Wouldn't you call him a bad boy, Uncle Wiggily?"

"Most surely I would," answered the rabbit gentleman. "But why does he do it? You don't crow over him; do you, Charlie?"

"No, indeed," answered the rooster boy. "I only crow to warn Arabella when I see that fellow coming, to tell her to run and hide under a bush."

"And I don't pick him, or scratch gravel at him or anything like that," cackled the little hen girl. "I wish he'd let us alone, Uncle Wiggily."

"We came over to see if you could think up a way to make him stop," crowed Charlie. "Can you?"

"Hum! I'll try," promised the bunny gentleman, twinkling his pink nose like the frosting on top of an orange shortcake. "Suppose we go look for this boy," went on Uncle Wiggily. "So I'll know him when I see him."

"I can show you his house," offered Charlie. "But we'll have to be careful. For if he sees us he'll peg things at us."

"Let us hope not," murmured Uncle Wiggily.

But it was a vain hope, as they say in fairy books. For after Uncle Wiggily, Charlie and Arabella had gone to the other side of a forest, there, all of a sudden, they saw the boy.

"Hi! There are those funny dressed-up chickens!" shouted the boy, who had red hair, and a face full of freckles. "And there's a rabbit with them, all dressed up in a tall silk hat! Oh, my! What style! I'm going to see if I can knock his hat off with a stone! I'm going to peg rocks at 'em!"

"See! What did I tell you?" cackled Arabella, who could understand boy talk, as could also Charlie and Uncle Wiggily.

"Bang!" bounced a stone on Uncle Wiggily's tall silk hat, sending it spinning through the air.

"Ha! Ha!" laughed the boy, as he picked up another stone. "I'm a good shot, I am!"

"I should call that rather a *bad* shot—for my hat," remarked Uncle Wiggily, as he picked up his silk tile and hopped toward the bushes. "Come on, Arabella and Charlie!" called the bunny gentleman. "This boy is acting just as you said he did. I must think up some way of teaching him a lesson!"

The little hen girl and rooster boy scooted under the bushes, and only just in time, for the boy threw many more stones, and one struck Charlie on the comb. Not the comb that he used to make his feathers smooth, but the red comb on his head—one of his ornaments; his tail feathers being others.

"Hi, fellows! Come on chase the funny chickens and the dressed-up rabbit!" cried the boy. But though some of his chums ran up, as he called, with sticks and stones, Uncle Wiggily, with Charlie and Arabella, managed to hide away from the thoughtless lads. For they were thoughtless. They didn't think that stones hurt animals.

"Yes, I certainly must teach that boy a lesson," said Uncle Wiggily.

"I—I wish he'd catch the chickenpox!" crowed Charlie. "Or maybe the roosterpox! Then he'd have to stay in and couldn't chase us!"

"I wouldn't care if he had the mumps and toothache at the same time!" cackled Arabella.

For several days Uncle Wiggily watched for a chance to teach the thoughtless boy a lesson, and at last it came. The bunny gentleman was out hopping in the woods one morning when he met Charlie and Arabella fluttering along the forest path.

The boy was asleep under a tree———

"Oh, Uncle Wiggily!" said Arabella in a cackling whisper. "That boy is asleep now, on a bed of moss under a tree. He's sleeping hard, too, for Charlie and I went close to him and he didn't awaken. Maybe you can do something to him now."

"Maybe I can," said Uncle Wiggily. "I'll go see!"

He hopped through the woods with the chicken children, and soon came to where the boy was asleep under a tree. It was a pine tree, with sticky gum oozing from the trunk and branches. And as soon as the bunny gentleman saw this gum he whispered:

"I have an idea! I'll teach this boy a lesson."

"How?" asked Charlie.

"I'll make him think he has the chicken-pox, or something worse," answered the bunny, with a silent laugh.

"Goodie!" cackled Arabella.

"Ha! Ha!" crowed Charlie.

"Quiet now, chicken children," whispered Uncle Wiggily. "Each of you pull me out a few loose feathers."

Charlie and Arabella did this. Then the bunny uncle took some of the soft gum from the pine tree, and put spots of it on the face and hands of the sleeping boy. Though he stirred a little, the boy did not awaken.

When the boy was well spotted with the sticky gum, Uncle Wiggily took the chicken feathers that Charlie and Arabella had plucked, and fastened these feathers on the boy's face and hands in the gum.

"Oh, how funny he looks!" softly cackled Arabella.

"Hush!" cautioned Uncle Wiggily, putting his paw on his pink, twinkling nose. "Let him sleep!"

Drawing back into the bushes, Uncle Wiggily, Charlie and Arabella waited for the boy to awaken, which he did pretty soon. He turned over, sat up and stretched. Then he looked at his hands, and saw chicken feathers stuck on them.

"Oh! Oh!" cried the boy. "What has happened to me?"

He jumped to his feet and caught sight of himself in a spring of water that was like a looking glass.

"Oh! Oh!" cried the boy again. "This is terrible! Oh, my face!"

Home he ran through the woods, while Charlie and Arabella laughed to see him go.

"Oh, Mother! Mother! Look at me!" cried the boy. "I'm all feathers! I must have the chicken-pox!"

"Goodness me, sakes alive and a basket of eggs!" exclaimed the boy's mother. "You must have gone to sleep in a hen's nest! But you haven't the chicken-pox! The chicken-pox is spots like the measles, but you are covered with *feathers!*"

"But how did I get this way?" asked the boy, as he pulled off some of the feathers. "I wasn't like it when I went to sleep in the woods."

"Maybe a fairy did it," spoke his little sister, who believed in them.

"Pooh! There aren't any fairies!" sneered the boy. "I guess it was that hen and rooster I stoned."

"Did you do that?" asked his mother. "Did you?"

"A—a little!" stammered the boy.

"Well, it isn't any wonder you're this way, then," Mother said. "And, for all I know, you may get the real chicken-pox!"

And, as true as I'm telling you that boy did! But he was not made very ill, for some reason or other. Perhaps because he had to be washed so clean, to get off the sticky pine gum and the feathers, the chicken-pox didn't go in very deeply.

At any rate, when the boy was all well again, he threw no more stones at Charlie or Arabella.

"You cured him, Uncle Wiggily!" crowed the rooster boy.

And I really think the bunny did. So if toy balloon doesn't take the spout off the teakettle to blow beans through at the egg beater, I'll tell you next about Uncle Wiggily's Hallowe'en.

STORY XX

UNCLE WIGGILY'S HALLOWE'EN

HOPPING along under the bushes one day, near the edge of the forest nearest to where lived the real boys and girls, Uncle Wiggily Longears, the bunny rabbit gentleman, heard two boys talking together.

"We'll put a tick-tack on her window," said the First Boy.

"And she'll be scared stiff!" said the Second Boy. "Oh, what fun we'll have this Hallowe'en!"

"Hum!" thought the bunny rabbit gentleman to himself, after hearing this. "It may be fun for *you*, but how about whoever it is you're going to scare stiff? I only hope it isn't my nice muskrat lady housekeeper, Nurse Jane Fuzzy Wuzzy!"

Uncle Wiggily twinkled his pink nose, and listened with both ears.

"Yes," went on the First Boy, "we'll have a lot of fun this Hallowe'en with tick-tacks and the like of.that! And we'll put on false faces so the Little Old Lady of Mulberry Lane won't know us!"

"Oh ho! So that's the one they're going to play tricks on; is it?" thought Uncle Wiggily to himself. "The Little Old Lady of Mulberry Lane! I know her—poor creature; she lives all alone, and she may have a cupboard, like Old Mother Hubbard, but she hasn't a dog or a bone. I suppose," thought Uncle

136

Wiggily, "that Jackie or Peetie Wow Wow would stay with her, if she wanted them. I must see about it.

"But, first of all, I must plan some way so these mischievous boys won't put a tick-tack on the window of the Little Old Lady of Mulberry Lane. I know what tick-tacks are!"

And well Uncle Wiggily knew, for sometimes the boys and girls of Woodland, near the Orange Ice Mountains, where the bunny had built his hollow stump bungalow, put one of the scary things on his window. That is, they were scary if you didn't know what they were, but Uncle Wiggily did.

Oftentimes Sammie Littletail, the rabbit, or Johnnie and Billie Bushytail, the squirrels, would take some string, a pin and an old nail, or little stone, and make a tick-tack. They fastened a short piece of string to the pin, and on the other end of the string they tied a dangling stone. When it grew dark the animal chaps would sneak up to Uncle Wiggily's window, and stick the pin in the wooden sash so the stone, or nail, hung dangling down against the glass. Then they would tie the long string, or thread, about half way down on the short cord and hide off in the bushes, with one end of the long string in their paws.

From their hiding place the animal boys would pull the long string. The pebble, or stone, would rattle against Uncle Wiggily's window, making a sound like:

"Tick! Tack!"

That's how it got its name, you see.

"So they are going to play tick-tack on the Little Old Lady of Mulberry Lane; are they?" said Uncle Wiggily to himself, as the two boys walked away. "Well, I must try to stop them!"

Mulberry Lane was a street near the forest where the bunny gentleman lived in his hollow stump bungalow, and the Little Old Lady was the only one whose house was built there. The bunny liked the Little Old Lady, for in winter she scattered crumbs for the birds.

Uncle Wiggily hopped home to his hollow stump, and from the attic he took down one of his old, tall silk hats.

"What in the world are you doing, Uncle Wiggily?" asked Nurse Jane. "Do you think it is April Fool, and are you going to wear an old hat so the animal boys won't play tricks on you?"

"Well, not exactly," the bunny answered. "I'll tell you later, Miss Fuzzy Wuzzy—if it works."

"Hum!" said the muskrat lady housekeeper, as she saw Mr. Longears put in his pocket some pieces of white paper and a pot of paste. "I do believe he's going to fly a kite—and on Hallowe'en of all nights!"

For it quickly became Hallowe'en night. As soon as the dusky shadows of evening began to fall, strange figures flitted to and fro, not only in the woods of the animal folk, but on the other side, in the village where the real boys and girls lived.

Real boys, with the heads of wolves, the faces of clowns and some as black as the charcoal-man skipped here and there, ringing doorbells, outlining in chalk on the steps something that looked like an envelope, or else they tapped on windows with long sticks so that when the windows were opened no one could be seen.

Uncle Wiggily, hopping off through the darkness toward the edge of the forest, carried with him one of Nurse Jane's old brooms, an old, tall silk hat and a coat the bunny gentleman had, long ago, tried to throw in the rag bag. Only Miss **Fuzzy Wuzzy** wouldn't let him.

"I'll mend it, sew on some new buttons and it will be as good as ever," she said. Well, Uncle Wiggily found this coat and took it with him.

"I'll stop those boys from putting a tick-tack on the window of the Little Old Lady of Mulberry Lane," thought the bunny as he hopped along. "I'll tick-tack them!"

He kept in the shadows of the trees so none of the animal children saw him. But the bunny gentleman saw them. He saw Neddie Stubtail, the boy bear, dressed up like the Pipsisewah. And Billie Wagtail, the goat, had on a false face just like the skinny Skeezicks.

Here and there animal girls were hurrying to Hallowe'en parties. Lulu and Alice Wibblewobble, the ducks, were giving one, and Baby Bunty, the little rabbit girl, had been invited to "bob" for carrots at the house of Buddy and Brighteyes, the guinea pigs.

Jackie and Peetie Bow Wow, who were dressed in clown suits, hurrying to have fun with Johnnie and Billie Bushytail, the squirrels, caught sight of Uncle Wiggily.

"Come and have some Hallowe'en fun with us!" barked Jackie.

"I will in a little while," promised the bunny.

On and on he hopped, and soon he came to the house of the Little Old Lady of Mulberry Lane. The bunny could look in her window and see her reading a book by the light of a candle.

"I'll hide under her window," thought the bunny, "and when those boys come with the tick-tack—well, we'll see what happens!"

Uncle Wiggily did not have long to wait. Pretty soon he heard a rustling in the bushes and some whisperings.

"Here they come!" thought Mr. Longears. He put the extra tall silk hat on top of the broom, and fastened his old coat to the handle, on a cross-stick he had nailed there. Then, taking the pieces of white paper from his pocket, Uncle Wiggily pasted them on the shiny part of the old silk hat in the shape of a grinning Jack o' Lantern face. Then the bunny crouched down behind the bushes with the scarecrow he had made.

"You sneak up and fasten on the tick-tack," whispered one boy, "and I'll pull the string so it will rattle and scare the Old Lady stiff!"

"I want to pull the string, too!" said the other boy.

"Yes, you can, after you fasten on the tick-tack."

"Well, give it here then," said the second boy.

They were so close to the bush, behind which Uncle Wiggily was hidden, that the bunny could have reached out and touched them with his paw if he had wished.

But he didn't do that. Instead, Uncle Wiggily suddenly lifted up the broom, dressed as it was in the old coat and the tall hat with the grinning, white paper face like a Jack o' Lantern.

"Boo-oo-oo-bunk!" groaned the bunny rabbit, scary-like.

The boys, who were just getting ready to frighten the Little Old Lady of Mulberry Lane, jumped up in fright themselves. They saw the queer face laughing at them.

"Oh, it's a Hallowe'en hobgoblin! A hobgoblin!" cried one boy.

"Come on! Come on!" shouted the other. "Let's get out of here!" And dropping string, tick-tack and everything, away they ran. They never knew that it was only a bunny rabbit gentleman who had surprised them.

"Ha! Ha!" laughed Uncle Wiggily, as he peered out from behind the broomstick and the scary tall-hat creature he had made. "I guess they won't bother the Old Lady now!"

The Little Old Lady of Mulberry Lane laid aside the book she had been reading and opened her door.

"Is anybody there?" she gently asked, looking out over her dark garden. "Seems to me I heard a noise-like. Is anybody there, trying to play Hallowe'en tricks on a poor, lone body like me? Anybody there?"

No one answered—not even Uncle Wiggily—for he couldn't speak real talk, you know. But he heard what the Old Lady said.

"Nobody there! I guess it must have been the wind," said the Little Old Lady of Mulberry Lane, as she shut the door.

But we know it wasn't the wind; don't we?

Then the bunny hopped back to his own part of the forest, to have Hallowe'en fun with the animal boys and girls. The frightened boys ran home and jumped into bed. And if the piano key doesn't unlock the door of the phonograph, and let all the music run down the pussy cat's tail, you may next hear of Uncle Wiggily and the poor dog.

STORY XXI

UNCLE WIGGILY AND THE POOR DOG

ONCE upon a time there was a dog so poor that he had no kennel to sleep in. He made his bed in old boxes and barrels along the street, or behind stores. And as for things to eat— that poor dog thought himself lucky if he found a bone without any meat on it! Oh, he was dreadfully poor, was that dog!

He had no collar to wear, though of course he did not miss a necktie, for dogs never wear those. But when this dog saw other dogs, with shiny brass or nickel collars around their necks, when he saw some of them riding in automobiles as he splashed through the mud, and when he looked over in yards and saw some dogs gnawing juicy, meaty bones in front of their warm kennels—this poor dog sometimes felt sad.

"I don't see what use I am in this world," thought the poor dog, as he chased away a tickling fly who wanted to ride on his tail. "I certainly can't help anyone, for I can hardly help myself! I think I'll go off in the woods and get lost! Yes, that's what I'll do," barked the poor dog. "Get lost!"

Perhaps if he had had a good breakfast that morning, with a biscuit or two, or even a slice of puppy cake, he might have been more happy. As it was, after crawling out of an empty rain-water barrel, where he had slept all night, and after finding only a small bone for his breakfast, this dog went off to the woods.

142

"Good-bye, everybody!" he softly barked, as he stood on the edge of the forest, and looked back toward the village he was leaving. But there was no one even to bark a farewell to him. All alone the poor dog started into the woods. "Good-bye!" he whined.

Now in this same forest, on the opposite side from the trees nearest the village, stood the hollow stump bungalow of Uncle Wiggily Longears. And this same morning that the poor dog decided to lose himself, the bunny rabbit gentleman started out with his tall, silk hat, his red, white and blue striped rheumatism crutch, and his pink twinkling nose to look for an adventure.

"Keep your eyes open for the Woozie Wolf or the Fuzzy Fox!" called Nurse Jane, the muskrat lady housekeeper as Mr. Longears hopped away.

"I will!" promised the bunny uncle.

Uncle Wiggily hopped along and along and along, looking behind bushes and rocks for an adventure when, all of a sudden, he saw a sort of hole down in between two logs.

"Perhaps there is an adventure down in there for me," said the rabbit gentleman. "I'll poke my paw down in and find out. This hole isn't large enough to be the den of the Fox or Wolf."

Uncle Wiggily thrust one of his forepaws down into the hole, and began feeling around between the logs. He touched something soft and fuzzy, and he was just beginning to think that perhaps Baby Bunty was hiding down there so he couldn't tag her when, all of a quickness, those logs rolled together. Before Uncle Wiggily could pull out his paw it was caught fast, and there he was, held just as if he were in a trap.

"Oh, my goodness me, sakes alive, and a basket of soap bubbles!" cried the bunny rabbit gentleman. "I'm caught! How dreadful! I must get out!"

Well, he pulled and he pulled and he pulled, but still his paw was held fast. He scrabbled around among the dried leaves, he tried to lift one log off the other with his rheumatism crutch, and he tried to gnaw a hole in the top log that held him fast. But it was all of no use.

"Oh, I'm afraid I'll have to stay here forever, unless I get help!" thought Uncle Wiggily. "But I must call for aid! Perhaps Grandpa Goosey, or Nurse Jane Fuzzy Wuzzy, will hear me!"

"Who calls for help?"

Uncle Wiggily stopped his pink nose from twinkling, so that he could call more loudly, and then he shouted:

"Help! Help! Help!"

For a time there was no answer, only the wind blowing among the leaves of the trees. And then, all at once, there was a rustling in the bushes and a voice asked:

"Who calls for help?"

"I do," answered Uncle Wiggily. "Oh, even if you are the Woozie Wolf or the Fuzzy Fox, please help me!"

"I am neither the Wolf nor the Fox," was the answer. "I am only a poor dog who came to this forest to lose himself. I never have been able yet to help anyone."

"Well, perhaps you can help me," said Uncle Wiggily, as cheerfully as he could speak. "Come here and see where the logs have fallen on my paw, holding me fast."

So the poor dog, with his ragged clothes which made him look almost like a tramp, came through the bushes, close to Uncle Wiggily.

"My, but you're stylish!" said the dog, as he saw Uncle Wiggily's tall, silk hat.

"That isn't anything," sadly said the bunny rabbit gentleman. "Tall hats do not make for happiness. I'd rather have on an old, ragged cap, like yours, and be free, than wear a diamond and gold crown like a king and be held fast here."

"Yes, it isn't fun to be caught in a trap," barked the poor dog. "But I think I can gnaw through one of those logs and set you free."

Then he began to gnaw. He gnawed and he gnawed and he gnawed, and, in a little while, one of the logs was cut in two, just as if it had been sawed, and Uncle Wiggily could pull out his paw.

"I can't tell you how thankful I am," said the bunny to the dog. "What fine, strong white teeth you have. How did you get them?"

"From gnawing bones without any soft meat on them, I suppose," answered the dog. "Poor dogs must have strong teeth, or they would starve. Rich dogs, who get soft food, can afford to have soft teeth."

"Well, then I am very glad you are a poor dog!" laughed Uncle Wiggily.

"You are?" barked the other, in great surprise.

"Certainly; of course I am!" exclaimed the bunny. "Just think! Suppose you had been one of those rich dogs, with soft, crumbly teeth! You would not have been able to gnaw through the log and I would still be held fast."

"Yes, that's so," agreed the dog, wagging his tail. "I never thought of that."

"Then be thankful, as I am, that you are poor, and have strong teeth," went on Mr. Longears. "You have been of great help to me."

"Have I?" barked the dog. "Then I am very glad! I never before helped anyone. I thought I was too poor!"

"Well, you aren't going to be poor any more," went on the bunny rabbit gentleman. "Come to the woods and live near my hollow stump bungalow. I have a friend, Old Dog Percival, who will let you stay in his kennel. He is rich!"

"Oh, that makes me very happy!" said the dog, who used to be poor. "I have always wanted a kennel to live in!"

Then he went home with the bunny rabbit. And, though he never became a very rich dog, still he had a warm kennel, which Percival shared with him, and he always had enough to eat; and he became great friends with Mr. Longears and Nurse Jane.

So this teaches us that even if a lollypop has a stick this does not mean it needs a whipping. And if the sunflower doesn't shine so brightly in the eyes of the potato that it can't see to get out of the oven, I'll tell you next about Uncle Wiggily and the rich cat.

STORY XXII

UNCLE WIGGILY AND THE RICH CAT

ONCE upon a time there was a very rich cat, but with all she had she was not happy. She owned an automobile and kept a little mouse servant girl to wait on her. And an old gentleman rat did all the heavy work around the house, such as putting out the ashes and cutting the grass.

"Heigh-ho!" sighed the rich cat lady one morning, after she had lapped up some thick, heavy cream, which was left on her doorstep each day. "Heigh-ho! I am so tired!"

"Tired of what?" squeaked the little mouse servant, as she brought a paper napkin for the rich cat to wipe the cream from her whiskers. Even though she was well-off, the cat lady had whiskers, and she was very proud of them.

"Oh, I am tired of sitting around doing nothing!" purred the rich cat.

"Then why not go for a ride in your auto?" asked the poor little mouse servant girl.

"I am tired of that, too," spoke the rich cat. "It is the same old thing every day! Dress and go out. Come back and dress to eat! Dress to go out again! Come back and undress to go to bed and get up in the morning to dress and do it all over again! I—I'd like to have an *adventure!*" mewed the cat lady.

"Oh, mercy! An *adventure!*" squeaked the mouse. "Never!"

"Yes," went on the cat, "a real, exciting adventure. I saw a poor dog the other day—at least he used to be poor, and he is far from rich now. But he looked so well, and so lively, with such strong, white teeth! I heard him telling another dog he had had a most wonderful adventure in the woods with an old rabbit gentleman named Uncle Wiggily. I quite envied that poor dog!"

"Oh, and you so rich!" murmured the mousie girl.

"I don't care!" mewed the wealthy cat lady. "I'd almost be willing to be poor if I could have an adventure. Come, I'll go for a ride in the auto. It will be better than dawdling around the house."

So the cat lady ordered out her auto, with the rat gentleman to drive it, and the little mousie girl to sit beside her on the cushioned seat.

"Where shall I drive to, Lady Cat?" asked the old gentleman rat chauffeur.

"Oh, anywhere—to the woods—the fields—anywhere so that I may have an adventure—I don't care!" mewed the rich cat.

So the rat gentleman drove the auto through the village, and out into the forest. At first the roads were very good, but at last they became bumpy, and the cat lady and mousie girl were much shaken up and jiggled about, not to say joggled.

"Do you want to go on?" asked the rat.

"Oh, yes," answered the cat. "It shakes up my liver, and I seem to be feeling more hungry. Go on, perhaps I shall find an adventure."

The auto lurched and bumped on a little farther and, all of a sudden there was a crash.

"Oh!" screamed the little mousie girl.

" What is the matter?" asked the cat lady, looking through her fancy glasses.

"We have had an accident," answered the gentleman rat. "The auto is broken, and I shall have to go for help."

"Let us go, also," squeaked the mousie girl. "We don't want to stay here in the woods alone."

"*You* may not want to," said the cat with a smile. "But *I* am going to. Run along with Mr. Rat, Miss Mouse, and get help. I'll stay here!"

So the rich cat lady was left alone, sitting in the auto, one wheel of which was broken, while the rat gentleman and mousie girl went to look for a garage where they could get help.

"Perhaps this is the start of an adventure," thought the cat.

A moment later she hear a rustling in the bushes, and out popped a strange dog. Now the rich cat lady knew some rich dogs who wore silver and gold collars, and were friends of hers. She was not afraid of them. But this was a dog without any collar, though he had on a suit of clothes. And, when the cat lady looked a second time, she saw that it was a boy dog and not a grown man dog.

"Bow! wow!" barked the boy dog. "You're a strange cat! What are you doing in these woods? Hi, Jackie!" howled the dog. "Come help me chase this strange cat up a tree!"

"All right, Peetie! I'm with you!" answered a voice, and out of the bushes came another boy dog. The two dogs rushed at the cat lady.

Now she might not have been afraid of *one* boy dog, but when *two* of them leaped toward her, this was enough to frighten almost any pussy! Don't you think so?

"Meaouw! Mew! Mee!" cried the cat, and before she knew it she was climbing a tree. Up she scrabbled, her claws tearing off bits of bark, until she was perched on a limb, high above her auto and the barking dogs down below.

"My goodness me, sakes alive, and a liver cream puff!" said the excited rich cat lady to herself, her heart beating like an alarm clock. "This is dreadful! To think of me, a wealthy cat, being chased up a tree by two poor dogs! What will my friends think?"

Then she looked down at the dogs and said:

"Run away if you please, little puppy boys!"

"No! No!" they barked. "Bow! Wow!"

"You run and tell him," said one puppy to the other. "Tell him there's a strange cat in his woods. I'll stay here at the foot of the tree so she can't get down until you come back with him!"

"I wonder whom they are going to bring back?" thought the rich cat up the tree. And she could not help laughing a little as she thought how strange she must look. "The mouse servant and rat chauffeur will be surprised when they come back and see me here," thought the cat.

One little puppy dog boy ran away, while the other remained on guard at the foot of the tree.

"May I come down?" asked the cat lady.

"No, indeed!" growled the dog, though he did not speak impolitely. "You must stay up there!"

"Dear me!" thought the cat lady. "This is quite an unexpected adventure!"

All of a sudden she saw the puppy at the foot of the tree jump up. At the same time there was a rustling in the bushes, and along came the other puppy, with an old gentleman rabbit, who wore a tall silk hat, who had a pair of glasses on his pink, twinkling nose and who walked with a red, white and blue striped rheumatism crutch.

"There she is, Uncle Wiggily!" barked a puppy dog. "We saw her in your woods, and chased her up a tree until you could look at her. Maybe she is the Woozie Wolf or the Fuzzy Fox, dressed up like a cat."

"Indeed I am not," said the rich pussy lady up the tree. "I am the Rich Mrs. Cat, and my auto has broken. When my mousie servant girl and the rat gentleman who drives my car return, they will tell you I never harm rabbits. But are you Uncle Wiggily Longears?" she asked.

"Yes," answered the bunny, "I am. And I know you, Mrs. Cat. I heard about you from the poor dog. I am very sorry Jackie and Peetie Bow Wow chased you up a tree. They meant no harm."

"I am sure they did not," mewed the cat politely.

"But they are always on the lookout so nothing will happen to me," went on Uncle Wiggily. "I would get up and help you down, only I can't climb a tree."

"Oh, I can easily get down," said the cat lady, and she did, though her rich clothes were rather ruffled. But she had plenty of money to buy more. So don't worry about that.

"Make yourself at home in these woods—the animal folk

call them mine," said Uncle Wiggily kindly. "I am sorry you had this trouble. Now I must hop away. I hope your auto will soon be mended. Come, Jackie and Peetie, if you want to help me."

"Where are you going?" asked the rich cat.

"To help a poor cat family," said Uncle Wiggily. "The cat gentleman of the house has been out of work a long time, his wife is ill and he has a number of little kittens. I was on my way to see the family when Jackie came to tell me you were up a tree."

"Well, I'm down the tree now," laughed the rich cat lady. "And will you please let me help this poor family? I have a lot of money—see!" and she showed a purse full of golden leaves which the animal folk use for money. "I can buy them food, and if Mr. Cat wants work, let him take my auto, after it is fixed, and use it for a jitney."

"What!" cried Uncle Wiggily. "Aren't you going to use that fine car any more? All it needs is a new wheel."

"Give it to the poor cat," was the answer. "I am never going to ride in it again. I feel so much better since I came to the woods—and climbed a tree—that I am going to live here for the rest of my life. I'll buy a hollow stump bungalow near you, Uncle Wiggily. I know, now, I am going to be very happy."

"Well, you will make the poor cat family happy, at any rate," said Mr. Longears.

"And to make others happy is to be happy yourself," mewed the rich cat lady.

She went with Uncle Wiggily, Jackie and Peetie to the home

of the poor cat family, and when the worried cat gentleman heard that he was to have the auto for a jitney, with which he could make money, he was so glad he almost stood on his head. And his wife and the kitten children were glad also.

When the rat gentleman chauffeur and the mousie servant girl came back, in another auto, to take the rich lady home, she said:

"I am going to stay with Uncle Wiggily. From now on I am going to live in the woods and be happy and poor."

"Oh, my!" squeaked the mousie servant. "Just fancy!"

"I never heard of such a thing," said the rat gentleman. "You had much better come home and live as you did before."

But the cat lady would not change her mind, and she built herself a bungalow near Uncle Wiggily's, and lived there happily forever after.

So from this we may learn, if we will, that when a pail leaks it is best to have it mended. And if the hand-organ monkey doesn't take the squeak out of the rubber ball to make a tin horn for the rag doll, the next story will be about Uncle Wiggily and the horse.

STORY XXIII

UNCLE WIGGILY AND THE HORSE

NURSE JANE FUZZY WUZZY, the muskrat lady housekeeper for Uncle Wiggily Longears, the bunny rabbit gentleman, once baked a cherry pie, of which Mr. Longears was very fond. In fact, Miss Fuzzy Wuzzy baked *two* pies.

One she put upon the shelf for Uncle Wiggily's supper. The other pie Nurse Jane wrapped in a clean napkin, put it in a basket, and then she said:

"Come on, Uncle Wiggily. We will take this pie to Grandfather Goosey Gander."

"That will be fine!" exclaimed Uncle Wiggily. So he set off with Nurse Jane, over the fields and through the woods. "And perhaps we may have an adventure," said the bunny gentleman, hopeful-like.

"Well, if we do," spoke Nurse Jane, "I hope nothing happens to this cherry pie. I baked one for you, and the other especially for Grandpa Goosey. I shouldn't like the Fuzzy Fox, nor yet the Woozie Wolf, to get this pie."

"Nor I," said Uncle Wiggily. "And I don't believe Grandpa Goosey would, either."

The rabbit gentleman and Nurse Jane hopped along together, until, after a while, Uncle Wiggily saw a horse in a field.

"Look at that poor horse!" said the bunny gentleman, coming to a stop, and peeping over the top of his pink, twinkling nose. "There he stands, all day long, with nothing to eat but grass."

"What else would he eat?" asked Nurse Jane, suspiciously.

"I don't s'pose he ever had a cherry pie," went on Uncle Wiggily reflective-like. "Poor horse! Never had any cherry pie!"

"Wiggy!" exclaimed Nurse Jane, as she took a firmer hold of the basket handle. "If you are thinking of giving Grandpa Goosey's pie to that horse——"

"Well, that's just what I'm thinking of," answered Mr. Longears. "Here, Nurse Jane, please give me that pie. You may run back home and get the one you were saving for me to give to Grandpa Goosey. I'll call this pie mine, and I'm going to give it to the horse."

"Well, I never in all my born days," exclaimed Miss Fuzzy Wuzzy, "heard the like of that!"

Still she knew Uncle Wiggily meant to be kind, so she gave the bunny rabbit gentleman the basket with the pie inside, and started back for the hollow stump bungalow to get the other.

The bunny rabbit certainly was not selfish, whatever else he was.

"Hello, Horsie!" exclaimed Uncle Wiggily, as he hopped through the field where the big animal was eating.

"Hello," answered the horse. "Oh, it's Uncle Wiggily!" he went on, as he stopped cropping the grass and looked up.

"Did you ever eat a cherry pie?" asked the bunny rabbit, beginning to take the cloth off the one in the basket.

"Cherry pie? I don't believe I ever did," slowly answered the horse. "Cherry pie! Hum! No, I never tasted any."

"Wouldn't you like to?" asked the bunny. "I should think you would get tired of eating grass all day long."

"Well, grass is my food, and I like it," neighed the horse. "But I like some oats once in a while, and some bran. Yes, and I think I'd like some cherry pie, also."

"Here! Take this one! Nurse Jane can bake more!" said generous Uncle Wiggily, and he held out the pie.

"Oh, my! That's a fine one!" whinnied the horse. "That looks most delicious."

"And it tastes as delicious as it looks," went on the bunny. "I know Nurse Jane's pies. Take a bite!"

The horse did. One bit was all that was needed to enable him to eat the whole pie, for it was only rabbit size, of course, not as large as the pies your mother bakes.

"Um!" said the horse, as the red cherry juice ran down his lips. "That was a good pie! I could eat more!"

"I'm sorry, but that's the only one I have," spoke Uncle Wiggily. "Nurse Jane has gone to get mine, that she put in the cupboard, to give to Grandpa Goosey. But to-morrow I'll have her bake you a large pie."

Just then Nurse Jane came along, with the other pie in the basket, and Uncle Wiggily said:

"The horse ate that cherry pie, Miss Fuzzy Wuzzy, and liked it very much. I have told him you'd bake him a larger one."

"Well, I s'pose I can," said the muskrat lady, looking at Uncle Wiggily in a funny way. "I s'pose I can."

"You are very kind," neighed the horse. "If I could only do you some favor——"

But just then, all of a sudden, out from behind a bush jumped the bad old Woozie Wolf.

"Ah ha!" howled the Wolf. "This is the time I have caught Nurse Jane as well as Uncle Wiggily. I shall have four ears to nibble to-day!" and he looked hungrily at the bunny and muskrat lady.

"Do you mean to say you are going to hurt good, kind Uncle Wiggily, who has just given me a cherry pie?" asked the horse quickly.

"Of course I am!" growled the Wolf. "He gave me no pie! I'm going to nibble the bunny!"

"Well, I just won't let you!" said the horse.

"How are you going to stop me?" asked the Wolf.

"Well, I have big teeth," the horse said. "They are not as sharp as yours, for they do not need to be so that I may crop the grass. But I can bite you with them, just the same."

"Ho! Ho!" sneered the Wolf. "Two can play at that game! I can bite worse than you."

"That's so, he can," whispered Uncle Wiggily to the horse. "Be careful!"

"Well, then I'll *kick!*" said the horse. "I'll rear up on my front legs and kick you with my hind ones, Mr. Wolf, if you hurt Uncle Wiggily."

"But you have no sharp toe-nails, such as I have!" growled the Wolf. "I'll scratch you with my toe-nails if you kick me."

"That's right—he will!" whispered Nurse Jane.

"I'm afraid you cannot save us," sadly said the bunny gentleman to the kind horse.

"Yes, I can!" suddenly neighed the horse. "This Wolf can do some things better than I, but he cannot run as fast. Quick! Jump up on my back, Uncle Wiggily and Nurse Jane. I'll gallop and trot, I'll gallop and trot and I'll gallop and trot—until I take you far away from this bad animal!"

"Don't you dare take Uncle Wiggily away from me!" howled the Wolf, for well he knew he could not run as fast as the horse.

The wolf was left
far,
far,
behind.

"Yes, I shall! I'll save Uncle Wiggily!" whinnied the horse. "Up on my back! Quick!" he called to the bunny and Nurse Jane.

Up they leaped, before the Wolf could get them. Then the horse galloped and trotted, galloped and trotted and galloped and trotted, until the Wolf was left far, far behind. And, oh, how angry that Wolf was! And how he howled! I wish you could have heard him.

No, on second thought, it is just as well you didn't hear him. It was not very nice howling.

"There! Now you are safe, Uncle Wiggily and Nurse Jane," said the horse, as he stopped galloping and trotting, away over on the far side of the field, far, far from the Wolf.

"Thank you for saving us," spoke the bunny, as he and Nurse Jane slid off the horsie's back.

"I'll bake you the largest cherry pie that ever was," promised the muskrat lady, "just as soon as I take this one to Grandpa Goosey."

And she made such a large pie that it took the horse forty 'leven bites to eat it.

So everything came out all right, you see. And if the post-man doesn't try to slip a letter through the slot in the baby's penny bank, and make the five cent piece jump over the dollar bill, I'll tell you next about Uncle Wiggily and the cow.

STORY XXIV

UNCLE WIGGILY AND THE COW

THIS is a story about Uncle Wiggily and the cow. Not the cow with the crumpled horn, nor yet the one that jumped over the moon, when the dish ran away with the spoon.

This was a sort of a red cow which ate green grass and gave white milk that was churned into yellow butter to be eaten on brown bread. There is no use asking me about all those colors for I don't know—nobody knows. They're just there, and that's all there is about it.

Now for the story.

One day the bunny rabbit gentleman was hopping over the fields and through the woods on his way to the store for Nurse Jane Fuzzy Wuzzy. He was going to get his muskrat lady housekeeper a jug of molasses so Nurse Jane might make a cake.

Uncle Wiggily hopped on and on, wondering if he would have an adventure that day, and he was thinking how good the molasses cake would taste when, all of a sudden, down in a field he saw a red cow. Not exactly red like a rose, you understand, or red like a barn, but still somewhat between those colors—a brownish-red, I suppose it would be called.

"Moo! Moo! Moo!" called the cow, in such mournful tones that Uncle Wiggily right away said:

"Something must be the matter! I'm going down and see if I can help that poor cow!"

161

Down into the meadow hopped the bunny rabbit gentleman, and when he reached the cow he looked at her and she looked at him, and the bunny asked:

"What is the matter, Mrs. Cow?"

"Oh," was the sad answer, "I've lost the cud that I always chew, and now I don't know what to do! I'm so upset I'm sure I'll give sour milk to-night, instead of sweet!"

"That would be too bad," Uncle Wiggily remarked. "This cud of yours—may I ask what it is?"

"Well, it isn't gum, as many boys and girls suppose, when they see me chewing," spoke the cow lady. "My cud is a bunch of grass, which I crop and pull up by winding my tongue about it, for I haven't two sets of teeth as have many animals. I only have teeth on my upper jaw. On my lower jaw I have no teeth,

"Well! Well!" exclaimed Uncle Wiggily.

but the gums are very hard so I can chew grass, and that is what makes my cud. I only chew the grass a little bit, when I first pull it from the meadow. I swallow it down into my first stomach, and, when I have more time, I bring the cud of grass up into my mouth and chew it as long as I please, so it will be good for me to put into my last stomach."

"Well, well!" exclaimed Uncle Wiggily in surprise. "So you have two stomachs and only one set of teeth."

"Yes," went on the cow," but what is worrying me now is to know whether I lost my cud of grass in the meadow, after I had chewed on it a while, or whether it slipped down into my last stomach before it was time."

"What will happen if it did?" asked Uncle Wiggily.

"I'm afraid I'll have indigestion," the cow lady answered. "And that will make my milk bad and sour. Oh, dear! I wish I knew where my cud was!"

"How did you come to lose it—or miss it?" asked the bunny.

"Why, I was watching Bully and Bawly No-Tail, the two frog boys, hopping down by the brook," the cow lady said. "They were playing leap-toad, you know—or, perhaps, it was leap-frog; and Bully made such a funny jump over Bawly's back that I laughed right out loud. I was chewing my cud at the time, and when I stopped laughing I missed it. Now whether I swallowed it, or whether it dropped in the brook, I don't know. Isn't that dreadful?"

"Can't you tell by the way you feel—inside, you know," asked the bunny, "what became of your cud?"

"Not for some little time," answered the cow lady, "and then it will be too late. Oh, if only I could find my cud somewhere in this meadow I'd know I hadn't swallowed it, and I'd be all right."

"I know just how you feel," said Uncle Wiggily. "Once, when Susie Littletail, the rabbit, was a tiny baby, her mother gave her a big cake spoon to play with. She went out of the room, leaving Susie to play with the spoon, and when she came back it was gone."

"What was gone?" asked the cow lady, "Susie or the spoon?"

"The spoon," answered the bunny gentleman. "And as Susie was too little to talk, and tell where it was, her mother didn't know whether she had hidden, or dropped the spoon somewhere, or whether she had swallowed it."

"Just fancy!" mooed the cow. "How exciting! But what happened?"

"Why, finally," said Uncle Wiggily, "after I had hopped over to help, we found the spoon behind the piano where Susie had thrown it. Then we knew she hadn't swallowed it."

"And if I could find my cud I'd know I hadn't swallowed *that*," sadly said the cow lady.

"I'll help you look," offered Uncle Wiggily. "I'm a pretty good hopper, and I'll hop around the meadow and look for your cud of half-chewed grass."

The bunny set down his molasses jug and began looking all over the meadow for the cud. And the cow helped, but she could not move very fast. Besides, she was worried and nervous.

"Here it is! I've found it!" suddenly called Uncle Wiggily, and there on the grass, near the brook where the frog boys had been leaping, was the cow lady's cud.

"Oh, how glad I am to get it back!" she mooed as she began to chew it again. "Now my milk will be nice and sweet. You have done me a great favor, Uncle Wiggily. I hope I may do you the same some day."

"Pray do not mention it," said the bunny politely, as he hopped on with his molasses jug. "It was just a little adventure for me."

Uncle Wiggily hopped on to the store, had the jug filled with molasses and then went to his hollow stump bungalow.

"Well, you were gone a long time," said Nurse Jane. "I have been waiting to make the ginger cake."

"I had to help a cow lady find her lost cud," said the bunny.

"Oh, Wiggy! What next!" laughed Miss Fuzzy Wuzzy. "Helping cow ladies! Oh! Oh!"

"That's all right," the bunny said. "Perhaps some day a cow lady may help us."

"I don't see how she can," spoke Nurse Jane, as she started to make the cake. But pretty soon she called to the bunny who had gone to sit outside on a bench and warm his rheumatism in the sun.

"Oh, Wiggy!" exclaimed Nurse Jane. "I can't get the cork out of the molasses jug. It's in so tight! I can't pull it out, and if I break it, and push it inside, then the molasses won't run out. Oh, what a lot of trouble!"

"Let me try!" offered the bunny. But he could not get the cork out of the molasses jug either, not even with his red, white and blue striped rheumatism crutch.

"I guess I'll have to break the jug!" said the bunny at last.

"Oh, don't do that!" spoke a voice behind him, and, turning,

Uncle Wiggily saw the cow lady. "I am on my way home to be milked," she mooed, "and I saw you in trouble, so I came over. What's wrong?"

"We can't get the cork out of the molasses jug," answered Uncle Wiggily.

"Perhaps I can," said Mrs. Cow. "Please let me try."

"We have a corkscrew somewhere," remarked Nurse Jane, "but I can't find it."

"I shall not need it," went on the cow.

Then with one of her long, sharp horns she easily pried the cork out of the molasses jug, breaking nothing and making it very easy for Nurse Jane to pour out the sweet stuff for the ginger cake.

"Thank you, Mrs. Cow," said Uncle Wiggily, as the milk lady animal went on her way.

"Pray don't mention it!" mooed the cow. "Now we are even, as far as favors go!"

Uncle Wiggily looked at Nurse Jane, and the muskrat lady smiled at the bunny gentleman.

"You were right, Wiggly," spoke Miss Fuzzy Wuzzy. "I never thought a cow could help anyone, but this shows how little I know."

"That's all right!" laughed the bunny. "Mistakes will happen!"

So once again everything came out all right for the bunny gentleman, you see, and if the pussy cat doesn't make a popcorn ball out of snow, for the puppy dog to play beanbag with, you shall next hear about Uncle Wiggily and the camping boys.

STORY XXV

UNCLE WIGGILY AND THE CAMPING BOYS

"OH, Uncle Wiggily! What you think?" cried Baby Bunty one day, as she hopped up to the rabbit gentleman, who was pulling the weeds out of his carrot garden.

"What I think, Baby Bunty?" repeated Mr. Longears, smiling down one side of his pink, twinkling nose. "Well, I think lots of things, my little rabbit girl. But if you think I'm going to play *tag* with you this morning you are wrong. I haven't time!"

"Oh, I don't want you to play tag!" exclaimed Baby Bunty, though she was such a lively little tyke that she nearly always wanted Uncle Wiggily to play a game of some sort. "But there's something over in the woods," she went on. "What you think it is?" and she was quite excited.

"Something over in the woods, Baby Bunty?" asked Uncle Wiggily, as he looked at one of his carrots to see if the point needed sharpening; but it didn't, I'm glad to say. "Well, what's in the woods, Baby Bunty; the Fox, the Skeezicks or the Pipsisewah?"

"Neither one, Uncle Wiggily," answered the little rabbit girl. "But there's a lot of those funny animals you call 'boys,' and they're making a snow house, and maybe they'll try to catch you, or me or Nurse Jane," and Baby Bunty looked quite worried.

167

"A *snow* house this time of year! Tut! Tut! Nonsense!" laughed Uncle Wiggily. "This is summer and there isn't any snow with which to make houses."

"Well, these boys, in the woods, are making a *white* house, anyhow, Uncle Wiggily," spoke the little rabbit girl, who once had lived in a hollow stump, before she came to visit the bunny gentleman. "It's a white house, and there's a lot of boys, and they're cutting down wood, and making a fire and boiling a kettle of water and oh, they're doing lots of things! I thought I'd better come and tell you."

"Hum!" said Uncle Wiggily, straightening up to rest his back, which ached from pulling the weeds out of his garden. "Yes, perhaps it is a good thing you told me, Baby Bunty. I'll go have a look at the white house the boys are putting up."

Uncle Wiggily and Baby Bunty hopped through the woods, and soon they were near that side of the forest nearest the village where real boys and girls lived. Through the green trees gleamed something white, on which the sun shone as brightly as it does at the seashore.

"There's the house," said Baby Bunty, pointing with her paw off among the trees.

"Ho! That isn't exactly a *house!*" Uncle Wiggily told the little rabbit girl. "That's a white tent, and those boys must be camping there. Boys like to come to the woods to camp in the summer. We'll hop a little closer and listen. Then we can tell what they are doing."

"We mustn't let 'em see us!" whispered Baby Bunty. "Oh, no!"

"Well, no, maybe not first along," Uncle Wiggily agreed.

"But nearly all boys, especially the kind that go camping, are fond of animals, and will not hurt them. We will see what sort of boys these are, Baby Bunty."

So the bunny gentleman and the little rabbit girl hid behind the bushes and watched the camping boys, for that is what they were. They had come to spend a few weeks in the woods, living in a white tent which, at first, Baby Bunty thought was a snow house.

The boys had just come to camp, and the tent had been up only a little while. But already the lads had started a camp fire; and they had hung a Gypsy kettle over the blaze, and were cooking soup.

"Get some more water, somebody!" called one boy.

"And I'm not going to cut any more wood!" exclaimed another. "I've been cutting wood ever since we got here!"

"We'll take turns!" spoke a third boy.

"Look out! That soup's boiling over!" shouted a fourth.

"They're regular boys all right!" chuckled Uncle Wiggily, as he crouched under a bush with Baby Bunty. "They're so excited at coming to camp they hardly know what they're doing."

Uncle Wiggily and Baby Bunty could hear and understand what the boys said, though they themselves could not speak to the camping chaps. For a time the two rabbits watched the little lads, who were trying to get a meal. They made many mistakes, of course, such as getting the salt mixed up with the sugar, and they left the bread out of its tin box so it dried, for they had never been camping before.

"But they'll soon learn," said Uncle Wiggily.

"I hope they won't chase us, and throw stones at us," Baby Bunty remarked, as she and Mr. Longears hopped away.

"I think they are good boys," spoke the bunny gentleman.

And the camping boys were. When they had finished eating they scattered crumbs so the birds could pick them up. Larger pieces of left-over food were placed on a flat stump where the squirrels and chipmunks could get them.

Johnnie and Billie Bushytail, the two boy squirrels, saw some of this food as they were coming through the woods. The camping boys were away just then, so the squirrel chaps had no fear of going close to the white tent-house. Johnnie found a piece of bread and butter, and Billie picked up half a ginger snap.

Johnnie found a piece of bread and butter.

"That shows the camping boys are kind to animals," said Uncle Wiggily, when Johnnie and Billie told him what they had found. "I hope I may get a chance to do these lads a favor."

And Uncle Wiggily had this chance sooner than he expected.

For about a week the weather was most lovely for camping. The sun shone every day, the wind blew just enough to send the sailboat spinning about the lake and there wasn't a drop of rain.

It is rain which soaks most of the fun out of camping, just as rain takes away your fun at home. And these boys, never having camped in a tent before, gave no thought to storms.

One afternoon it began to rain. Uncle Wiggily, in his hollow stump bungalow, where he was reading the cabbage-leaf paper, heard the pitter-patter of the drops on the window, and looked up.

"Where is Baby Bunty, Nurse Jane?" asked the bunny gentleman

"Why, she hasn't come back from the store yet," answered the muskrat lady housekeeper.

"Did she take an umbrella?" asked Uncle Wiggily.

"No," replied Nurse Jane, "she did not."

"Then she'll get soaking wet!" exclaimed Mr. Longears. "I'll go after her with a toadstool."

You know in Woodland, near the Orange Ice Mountain, where Uncle Wiggily lived, toadstools were often used for umbrellas. Of course, some of the animal folk had regular umbrellas, but when they were in a hurry they could break off a big toadstool, or mushroom, and use that.

So Uncle Wiggily hopped out of his hollow stump bungalow, and. growing near his front gate, he found a big toadstool. Picking this, he held it over his head and hurried along through the rain to meet Baby Bunty, who had gone to the three and five-cent store for Nurse Jane.

Uncle Wiggily had to hop almost to the place where the tent of the camping boys stood before he met the little rabbit girl, half drenched.

"Oh, Uncle Wiggily! You ought to see!" cried Baby Bunty. "There is so much water around the tent that those nice boys will be washed away, I guess!"

"Water around their tent?" repeated the bunny gentleman. "You don't say so!"

"Yes," said Baby Bunty. "The rain is coming down so hard that it is running like a little brook around the tent. The boys are inside, and I heard them saying that the water would soon come up over the cots and they wouldn't have any dry place to sleep to-night!"

"Silly boys!" exclaimed Uncle Wiggily, holding the toad-stool umbrella over Baby Bunty. "They didn't know enough to dig a ditch around the outside of their tent to let the rain water run off. All campers do that, but as this is the first time these boys came to the woods I suppose they didn't know about it. Always dig a ditch, or trench, in the earth around your tent when you go camping, Baby Bunty."

"I will," promised the little rabbit girl, real serious like.

"But that isn't going to help the boys now," went on Uncle Wiggily. "I think I shall have to take a paw in this. They are good boys. and are kind to animals. I must do them a favor."

"But how can you?" asked Baby Bunty.

"Why, I, being a rabbit, am one of the best diggers in the world," went on Mr. Longears. "Still, I will need help to dig a ditch around the tent, as it is rather large. Hop home, Baby Bunty, and tell Sammie Littletail, Toodle and Noodle Flat-Tail, the beaver boys, and Grandpa Whackum, the old beaver gentleman, to please come here. With their help I can dig the ditch."

So Baby Bunty, taking the toadstool umbrella, hopped away, and Uncle Wiggily, to await her return, hid under a thick-branched pine tree which kept off most of the rain. The drops pelted down, and around the tent of the camping boys was almost a flood. Night was coming on, too, and before morning the water would rise up so high that it would wet the feet of the boys in their beds.

Pretty soon, just about dusk, when it was still raining hard, along came Sammie Littletail, the rabbit boy, Toodle and Noodle the beavers, with their broad, flat tails, and Grandpa Whackum, the oldest beaver of them all. Beavers just love to work in the water and they can dig dirt canals better than most boys.

"Lively now, my friends!" called Uncle Wiggily, coming out from under the pine tree. "We'll dig a ditch around the tent for the kind boys. They won't see us, as they are inside, and probably will not come out in the train."

So Uncle Wiggily, Sammie and the beavers began work. Quickly and silently they dug and dug and dug in the soft earth, piling the dirt to one side, and making a trench so that the rain water could run off into the brook. And soon the little pond that had formed around the tent of the camping boys had drained away.

"Now they will have no more trouble," said Uncle Wiggily, as he and his friends, all wet and muddy, finished the trench. "We can go home."

Home they went, through the rain, to get something to eat, and dry out. And in the morning, though it still rained, no water rose inside the boys' tent. And none came through the roof, for that was like an umbrella, the canvas cloth being stretched over the ridge-pole.

"Oh, look!" cried one boy, coming to the flap of the tent, as the front of the canvas house is called. "Some one has dug a ditch around our camp, and now we'll keep dry!"

"Why, it's a regular little canal!" exclaimed a second boy. "It wasn't there yesterday!"

"Who did it?" asked the other lads.

But none of them knew, and I hope you will not tell them, for I want to keep it a secret.

And when the rain stopped, the ground around the tent dried out very quickly because the proper ditch had been dug around it. And the camping boys put out on the flat stump many good things for the animal folk to eat. And the next time those boys went camping they knew enough to make a trench around their tent.

Now let me see; what shall we have next? Well, I think I shall tell you the story of Uncle Wiggily and the birthday cake —that is, I will if the snow-shovel doesn't make the coal-scuttle sneeze when they are playing tag down under the cellar steps.

STORY XXVI

UNCLE WIGGILY AND THE BIRTHDAY CAKE

"To-morrow is my birthday! To-morrow is my birthday! And I'm going to have a cake with ten candles on!"

A little girl sang this over and over as she danced around the house one morning.

"Ten candles! And they'll be lighted, and I can blow them out and cut the cake and pass it around; can't I, Mother?" asked the little girl.

"Yes, my dear," Mother answered. "But if you are going to have a birthday cake you must go to the store and get me some flour, sugar and eggs. I did not know I needed them, but I do, if you are to have a cake."

"Oh, of course I want a cake!" said the little girl. "It wouldn't be at all like a birthday without a cake! And ten candles on top, all lighted! Last year I only had nine candles. But now I can have ten! Ten candles! Ten candles on my birthday cake!" sang the happy little girl again and again. "Ten candles! Ten candles!"

"You had better go to the store, instead of singing so much!" laughed her mother. "Sing on your way, if you like. But don't forget the flour, sugar and eggs."

"I'll get them," said the little girl, and off she started, taking a short cut through the woods to reach the store more quickly.

These woods were the same ones in which Uncle Wiggily had built his hollow stump bungalow, and about the same time the little girl started off to get the things for her birthday cake the bunny rabbit gentleman stood on his front porch.

"Where are you going?" asked Nurse Jane Fuzzy Wuzzy, his muskrat lady housekeeper.

"Oh, just to hop through the forest, to look for an adventure," answered Mr. Longears. "I haven't had one since I helped dig the rain-trench about the tent of the camping boys."

"I should think that would be enough to last a long time," spoke Miss Fuzzy Wuzzy.

"Oh, no. I need a new adventure every day!" laughed the bunny, and over the fields and through the woods he hopped.

Now Uncle Wiggily had not gone very far before, all of a sudden, he stepped into a trap. It was a spring trap, set in the woods by some hunter who had covered it with dried leaves so it could not easily be seen. That's the way hunters fool the wild animals.

And, not seeing the trap, Uncle Wiggily hopped right into it.

"Snap!" went the jaws of the trap together, catching the poor bunny gentleman fast by one hind leg.

"Oh, my!" cried Mr. Longears. "I'm caught! But it is fortunate that it is a smooth-jawed trap, and not the kind with sharp teeth. If I could only get my leg loose I'd be all right; except that my paw might be lame and stiff for a few days. I must try to get out!"

Uncle Wiggily tried to pull his paw from the trap, but it **was** of no use. The spring held the jaws too tightly together. The bunny gentleman twinkled his pink nose as hard as he could. and he even tried to pry apart the trap jaws with his red, white and blue striped rheumatism crutch. But he couldn't.

"Oh, dear!" though Uncle Wiggily. "I must call for help. Perhaps Neddie Stubtail, the strong boy bear, will hear me. He could easily spring open this trap and set me free."

So the bunny gentleman called as loudly as he could:

"Help! Help!"

Of course he talked animal talk, and for this reason the little girl, who was going to have a birthday cake, with ten candles on it, did not know what Uncle Wiggily was saying. She heard him making a noise, though, for she passed the place where the bunny was caught in the trap, soon after the accident happened.

"I wonder what that funny noise is?" said the little girl, as Uncle Wiggily again called for help. "It sounds like some animal. I wish I understood animal talk!"

Uncle Wiggily wished, with all his heart, that the little girl could hear what he was saying, for he was calling for help. The bunny understood girl-talk, and he knew what this girl was saying, for she spoke her thoughts out loud.

"But she doesn't know what I want!" said poor Uncle Wiggily to himself. "She is sure to be good and kind, as all girls are, and if I could only get her to come over this way she might take me out of the trap."

The little girl, on her way home from the store, had come to a stop not far from Uncle Wiggily, but she could not see him because he was behind a bush.

"I must make some kind of a noise that she will hear," thought the bunny. Then he thrashed around in the bushes with his crutch, rattling the dried leaves and the green bushes, and the little girl heard this noise.

"Oh, maybe a bird is caught in a big cobweb!" said the little girl. "I'll get it loose—I love the birds!"

Putting down her bundle of flour, sugar and eggs on a flat stump, she made her way through the bushes until she saw where Uncle Wiggily was caught in the trap.

"I wish you would come to my birthday party!"

"Oh, what a funny rabbit!" cried the little girl as she looked at the bunny gentleman all dressed, as he always was when he went to look for an adventure. "He looks just like a picture on an Easter card!" laughed the little girl. "I wish I had him at my party!"

"Well, I wish she'd take this trap off my paw!" thought Uncle Wiggily, though of course he could say nothing, however much he could hear.

Then the little girl looked down among the leaves and saw where the trap pinched Uncle Wiggily.

"Oh, you poor bunny rabbit!" she cried. "I'll set you loose."

Very gently she pressed her foot on the spring of the trap, to open it. And when the jaws were opened Uncle Wiggily could lift out his paw, which he did. He hopped a little way over the dried leaves, limping a bit, for the pinching trap had pained him. Then, coming to a stop on a smooth, grassy place, the bunny leaned on his red, white and blue striped rheumatism crutch and, taking off his tall silk hat, he made a low and polite bow to the little girl.

"Thank you for having done me a great favor!" said Uncle Wiggily in animal talk. "I wish I could do one for you!"

But of course the little girl could not understand this bunny language, so she only laughed and said:

"Oh, what a dear, funny bunny! With a tall hat and everything! I wish you would come to my birthday party! I'm going to have a cake with ten lighted candles on!"

"Thank you, I'd like to come, but it is out of the question," answered Uncle Wiggily in his own talk. Then, with another low and polite bow, he hopped away.

The little girl picked up the things she had bought at the store and went home.

"You'll never guess what I saw in the woods," she told her

mother. "A bunny rabbit, all dressed in a black coat and red trousers, was caught in a trap, and I set him free!"

"Nonsense!" laughed Mother. "Whoever heard of a rabbit like that? You are so excited about your birthday cake that you were dreaming, I think!"

"Oh, no, Mother! I didn't dream!" said the little girl. "Really I didn't!"

"Well, never mind. Now we'll make your birthday cake," answered Mother.

The birthday cake was mixed and baked in the oven, and on top was spread pink frosting.

"We'll put the candles on to-morrow, when you have your party," Mother told the little girl.

To-morrow came, after a night in which Cora Janet, which was the little girl's name, had dreamed about riding in an air-ship, with a bunny gentleman dressed up like a soldier. In the afternoon many boys and girls came to Cora Janet's birthday party.

"Oh, how lovely everything is!" exclaimed a little boy, when he was given his second dish of ice cream.

"Wait until you see my birthday cake with ten candles on!" whispered Cora Janet.

When it was almost time to bring on the lighted cake, Mother called Cora Janet out into the kitchen.

"Did you get the candles, Cora?" Mother asked.

"Why, no!" the little girl answered. "I—I thought we had candles!"

"And I thought I told you to get them," Mother went on. "There isn't one in the house! I've looked everywhere. Never mind, perhaps I can borrow some next door. Go back to your friends."

"Oh, I do hope you can get candles!" sighed Cora Janet. "A birthday cake without candles will hardly be right!"

Mother asked the lady who lived next door, on one side, if she had any candles.

"Not a one, I'm sorry to say," was the answer.

Then Mother asked the lady on the other side.

"Oh, I never use candles," this lady replied, coming out on her back stoop to talk over the fence to Cora Janet's mother. "I'm so sorry!"

"Well, I guess they'll have to eat the cake without any birthday candles on," said Mother. "Cora Janet will be so disappointed, too, as she is such an imaginative child! Just fancy, Mrs. Blake, she came home yesterday, and told about helping out of a trap an old rabbit gentleman, with a tall silk hat!"

"The idea! She must have dreamed it!" said Mrs. Blake.

"No, she didn't dream it! That really happened!" said Uncle Wiggily to himself, who was just then hopping through the fields back of the house where Cora Janet lived. "So this is her home, is it?" went on the bunny gentleman to himself. "And she hasn't any candles for her birthday cake! Too bad!"

Uncle Wiggily had hopped along just in time to hear Cora Janet's mother asking for candles of the neighbors.

"It's so late that all the stores are closed," went on Mrs. Blake, "or I'd go get some candles for Cora."

"Never mind," spoke Mother. "She will have to bear her disappointment as best she can."

"No! That must not be!" said Uncle Wiggily to himself.

"I cannot give her real candles, but I can leave on her steps some slivers of the pine tree. They have in them pitch, tar and resin and will burn almost like candles. When I was a rabbit boy I often lighted these pine-tree candles."

Not far away were the woods, and, hopping across the field in the dusk of the evening, Uncle Wiggily, with his sharp teeth, soon gnawed off some pine-knot splinters from one of the trees. In olden times, when there were no electric or kerosene lamps, children used to study their lessons in front of the fireplaces, by these pine knots.

"These will do for birthday-cake candles," whispered Uncle Wiggily, as he hopped back to Cora Janet's house with a paw full of the pine knots. He put them on the stoop, and then, with his hind paws, he kicked some gravel from the front walk up against the dining-room windows.

"What's that?" asked Cora Janet, as she heard the noise.

"Some bad boys playing tick-tack," said one of the girls at the party. "They're playing tricks because they weren't asked."

"I'll see who it is," spoke Mother.

She went out on the porch. There she saw the pile of pine knot slivers. Having lived in the country when she was a girl, Mother knew that these bits of wood could be used for candles.

"Oh, now I can make the birthday cake blaze most brightly!" exclaimed Mother. Into the house she hurried. She stuck ten pine-knot slivers on the cake, for Uncle Wiggily had left a full dozen, not knowing exactly how old Cora Janet was. Then, when the pine knots were lighted, Mother carried the cake into the room where the boys and girls were wishing Cora Janet many happy returns for her birthday.

"Oh, where did you get the candles?" asked Cora.

"I guess the rabbit you dreamed you saw must have left them," answered Mother, in fun, of course, for she never thought that really could happen.

"Dream-candles or not, they are lovely!" murmured the little girl.

And everyone at the party said the same thing.

They watched Cora Janet as, one by one, she blew out the pine candles on her birthday cake. And when the last one flickered away, the cake was cut amid the joyous laughter of the boys and girls.

"Well, I'm glad I could do her a favor," said the bunny rabbit to himself, as hidden under the lilac bush, he heard and saw all that went on. "I shall always love Cora Janet!"

And he did.

So if the needle doesn't wink its eye when it sits on the sewing-machine to read the paper of pins, I'll tell you next about Uncle Wiggily and the New Year's horn.

STORY XXVII

UNCLE WIGGILY AND THE NEW YEAR'S HORN

CHRISTMAS had come and gone, and the next holiday for the boys and girls who lived in the village outside of Uncle Wiggily's forest was to be New Year's Day. I call it Uncle Wiggily's forest for on one edge of it the bunny rabbit gentleman had built himself a hollow stump bungalow. There he lived with Nurse Jane Fuzzy Wuzzy, his muskrat lady housekeeper.

On the farther side of the wood was the village where many real boys and girls had their homes. To them, as I say, Christmas had come and gone, bringing to most of them presents which they liked very much.

"I'm going to have a lot of fun on New Year's," said one boy to another as they were coasting on the hill the last day of the old year.

"What are you going to do?" asked the other boy.

"I'm going to blow the Old Year out and the New Year in," was the answer.

"Gracious me sakes alive!" thought Uncle Wiggily Longears, the bunny rabbit gentleman, who happened to be resting under a bush near where the boys were coasting down hill. "I hope he doesn't blow the Old Year so far away that the New Year will be afraid to come in," said Mr. Longears to himself. Then he listened again, for the boys were talking further.

"How you going to blow?" one lad wanted to know.

"With my Christmas horn," was the answer. "I got a dandy horn for Christmas. To-night is New Year's eve. My father said I could stay up late. At twelve o'clock the Old Year goes away and the New Year comes, and we're going to have a party at our house, and I'm going to blow my horn like anything!"

"So'm I," said several other boys.

"Where does the Old Year go when you blow it away?" asked a lad who had red hair and freckles.

"Oh, I don't know," answered the boy who had first talked of his Christmas horn. "It just goes—that's all! It disappears same as the hole in a doughnut when you eat it."

"You don't eat the *hole!*" declared another boy.

"Well, you eat all around it," was the answer, "and then there isn't any hole any more. It's the same with the Old Year. After twelve o'clock on December 31 there isn't any Old Year any more. It's January the first, and it's the New Year. I'm going to blow my horn loud! All the fellows are!"

"We will, too!" cried the rest of the boys.

But one lad, who had a clumsy, home-made sled on the hill, did not say he was going to blow the New Year in. He turned away as the other lads talked of their coming fun. Some one asked him:

"Are you going to watch the Old Year out, Jimmy?"

"No, I guess not," was the answer. "I'm going to sleep."

"The noise will wake you up," some one suggested.

"Well, then I'll go to sleep again," was the answer.

"I guess the reason Jimmy won't blow the Old Year out and the New Year in is because he hasn't any horn," said a boy with a fine new blue sled. "He didn't get hardly anything for Christmas."

"That's too bad!" softly spoke the lad who had first mentioned about blowing in the New Year. "Maybe I can find an old horn at my house, and I'll take it to him. If I could find two I'd take another to his sister. But I don't believe I can."

"Oh, won't we have fun, blowing the New Year in?" cried the boys, as they walked to the top of the hill so they might coast down. But Jimmy did not join in the joyous shout. He was a poor boy, and, as the others had said, he had not found much in his stocking at Christmas. Certainly there was no bright tooting horn!

"This is too bad!" thought Uncle Wiggily, as he hopped back to his hollow stump bungalow, after the coasting boys were out of the way so they would not see him. "I wonder how I could get a New Year's horn for that poor boy?"

The bunny gentleman was wondering about this, but he could not seem to think of any plan, when, as he was about to hop up his bungalow steps, he saw Billie Wagtail, the goat boy.

"Oh, Uncle Wiggily!" bleated Billie. "See my new horns!"

"Your new horns!" exclaimed Mr. Longears, turning toward the goat chap. "Are you going to blow the New Year in, also?"

"Yes, but not with these horns," went on Billie. "I mean, see the new horns on my head. I was ill, you know, and my old horns dropped off, and now I have these new ones," and he shook his head, on which were two long, curving sharp horns. "I'm going to blow the New Year in," bleated the boy goat, "but not on my head horns; on my Christmas tin horn."

"That's more than one boy whom I know about is going to

do," said Uncle Wiggily a little sadly. Then the bunny gentleman had a sudden thought. "Do you s'pose, Billie," he asked the goat boy, "that your old horns could be made into blowing ones for New Year's?"

"Why, yes, I guess so," Billie answered. "But you'd have to saw off one end to make a place to blow in. My horns are partly

"Oh, Uncle Wiggily!"
bleated Billy.
"See my new horns!"

hollow and if you blew in the little end, after making a hole there, the noise would come out the other end."

"Then I know what I can do!" exclaimed Uncle Wiggily. "Get me your old horns, Billie boy, and I'll fix them up for New Year's blowing. I know how to do it!"

The Wagtail goat chap gave the bunny gentleman the old horns. Uncle Wiggily took them into his bungalow, and he and

Nurse Jane washed them clean and polished them. Then, with her sharp teeth, the muskrat lady gnawed a little off the small end of each horn, so they could be blown through.

Uncle Wiggily made two wooden whistles and fastened one in the small end of each horn

"Now I'll try it, Janie," he said to Miss Fuzzy Wuzzy.

Uncle Wiggily blew into the small end of one horn. Out of the other end came a sweet tooting sound.

"Hurray!" cried the bunny gentleman. "These will be just right for New Year's! I'll take one to the poor boy and one to his sister. Then they can celebrate with their friends who have regular tin horns."

"It is very kind of you to be so thoughtful," said Nurse Jane.

"And it was kind of you to help me make the New Year's horns from Billie's old ones," spoke Uncle Wiggily, as he skipped along, for it was getting dark and soon the Old Year would go away—like the hole in the doughnut—and the New Year would come, to bring with it Fourth of July, birthdays and Christmas.

Up the steps of the house of the poor boy and girl who had no New Year's horns to blow hopped Uncle Wiggily. No one saw him in the dusk. He placed the horns on the doormat, tapped three times with his red, white and blue striped rheumatism crutch on the porch, and then hopped away.

"What was that?" asked the girl of the boy.

"I'll go see," he answered.

The boy opened the door and saw, in the light of the moon, which just then came from behind a cloud, the two goat horns made into New Year's "tooters."

"Oh, hurray!" shouted the boy, as he blew on one of the horns. "Now we can send the Old Year on its way and tell the New Year how glad we are to see him. Hurray!"

"And I can blow, too!" laughed the girl. "Hurray!"

Her brother gave her the other horn, and when twelve o'clock midnight came, the children blew on the tooters as loudly as they could. So did all the other boys and girls in the village; and the animal boys and girls in their nest-houses and burrows also blew on horns and wooden whistles to welcome the New Year.

All over the land the bells rang and horns were blown. Uncle Wiggily heard them in his hollow stump bungalow, and so did Nurse Jane.

"Happy New Year!" wished the muskrat lady.

"Happy New Year!" echoed the bunny gentleman.

The boy and girl, blowing Billie Wagtail's old horns, danced around their father and mother, wishing them a Happy New Year also.

"Where did you get the horns?" asked Mother.

"Oh, I guess Santa Claus dropped them, on his way back to the North Pole," answered the boy.

But we know better than that; don't we?

So, after all, everything came out right, and the boy and girl were very happy with their queer New Year's horns.

But if the Jumping Jack doesn't tickle the lollypop with the sharp end of the ice-cream cone, and make it fall off the stick, I'll tell you next about Uncle Wiggily's Thanksgiving.

STORY XXVIII

UNCLE WIGGILY'S THANKSGIVING

THERE came, one afternoon, a knock at the door of the hollow stump bungalow where Uncle Wiggily Longears lived.

"Do you s'pose that can be the Fuzzy Fox or the Woozie Wolf?" anxiously asked Nurse Jane, the muskrat lady housekeeper.

"No," answered the bunny gentleman. "They would not dare come boldly up to my bungalow, in broad daylight, though if it were night they might come sneaking along, trying to nibble my ears. I suppose this may be Sammie or Susie Littletail, or Johnnie or Billie Bushytail. I'll let them in."

But when Uncle Wiggily opened the door, in came rushing a great big turkey gobbler gentleman. In his bill he carried a basket in which set a dish filled with something red.

"I have it, Uncle Wiggily! I have it!" exclaimed the turkey. "I picked it up and ran away with it! Now they can't have any Thanksgiving and I'll be safe! Shut the door!" he gobbled, and setting the basket on the floor he scuttled behind a chair, while Nurse Jane and Uncle Wiggily were so surprised they hardly knew what to do.

"*What* in the world have you brought with you, Mr. Gobble Obble?" asked the bunny gentleman. Gobble Obble was the turkey's name.

"The *cranberry sauce*," was the answer. "At our house, where

I have been living, they are making a great fuss over Thanksgiving, which will happen in a few days.   They have been feeding me up to fatten me, and every day the Man would come out and look at me; though I didn't know what for until I heard the children talking about it."

"Talking about what?" Nurse Jane wanted to know.

"*Thanksgiving*," gobbled the turkey.   "This morning I heard the cook say: 'That gobbler is fat enough to roast, now.   I think I'll make the cranberry sauce.   It will be Thanksgiving soon!'

"Then," went on the turkey, "I knew why they had been feeding me things to make me fat!   You can't imagine how I felt! Well, the cook made the cranberry sauce.   She put it in a dish and set it out on the back steps to cool.   I watched my chance, picked it up and ran over here.   There's the cranberry sauce!" and Mr. Gobble Obble pointed to it with one wing.

"But why in the world did you bring away the cranberry sauce?   What good is that going to do you?" asked Uncle Wiggily, very much puzzled by the turkey's queer talk and actions.

"Listen," gobbled the turkey.   "I heard one of the children say that Thanksgiving wouldn't be Thanksgiving without *turkey and cranberry sauce!*   Then, thinks I to myself, if I run away, and take the cranberry sauce with me, there will be no Thanksgiving, and many poor turkeys will be glad of it."

"Ha! Ha! Ha!" laughed Uncle Wiggily, chuckling so hard that his pink nose twinkled like a lightning bug on Fourth of July.

"What's the matter?" asked Mr. Gobble Obble.   "Won't you be good enough to hide me and the cranberry sauce until after Thanksgiving?   Then I'll be safe."

"Of course you may stay here," said the bunny gentleman. "But the idea of thinking you can stop Thanksgiving by hiding yourself, or the cranberry sauce!"

"Can't I?" asked Mr. Gobble Obble, doubtful-like.

"Of course you can't!" exclaimed Mr. Longears. "Why, Thanksgiving doesn't mean just feasting on turkey, ice cream and cranberries!"

"It does at the house I ran away from," said Mr. Gobble Obble.

"Yes, and I suppose it does at many other houses," went on the bunny gentleman. "But Thanksgiving is really a time in which to be thankful for the things one has had to eat all the year—for that, and other blessings. The Pilgrim Fathers, who came over to live among the Indians, were thankful for even a little parched corn."

"What are Indians?" asked the turkey, who had never studied history.

"Wild men, who wore feathers such as yours," said Nurse Jane. "They are Indians."

"I'll tell you about the Indians some day," promised Uncle Wiggily. "Now we must talk more about Thanksgiving."

"I don't like to talk about it," sighed Mr. Gobble Obble. "It isn't a happy thing for me even to think about, much less talk about!"

"But you shouldn't have run away with the cranberry sauce," went on the bunny gentleman. "I'm afraid I shall have to ask you to take it back."

"All right—I will," promised Mr. Gobble Obble. "But I'll

go after dark, so the cook won't see me. Then I'll come here again and stay with you and Nurse Jane."

"Yes, do," invited the bunny. "Spend Thanksgiving with us."

So when it grew dark Mr. Gobble Obble picked up the basket of cranberry sauce in his bill, and went over the fields and through the woods to the village, where lived the real boys and girls and their fathers and mothers. Softly and silently, like the shadow of a feathered Indian, the turkey made his way to the back stoop. There he set down the cranberry sauce and scuttled over to Uncle Wiggily's hollow stump bungalow again.

Days and nights came and went, and then it was Thanksgiving.

"Very lucky am I to live to see this day," gobbled the turkey as he ate breakfast with Uncle Wiggily and Nurse Jane. "If I hadn't run away with the cranberry sauce I'd be roasting in the oven now!"

"Well, I'm glad you aren't," spoke the bunny. "Though of course it wasn't right for you to take the cranberry sauce."

"They'll have that for Thanksgiving, anyhow," remarked Nurse Jane. "But now, Wiggy," she went on, "if I get the baskets ready, will you start out with them?"

"Yes, Miss Fuzzy Wuzzy," answered the bunny gentleman, twinkling his pink nose.

"What baskets are you speaking of?" asked Mr. Gobble Obble, as he saw the muskrat lady putting carrot cakes, turnip flopovers and lettuce sandwiches up in little bundles.

"These are for the poor folk of animal land," answered Uncle Wiggily. "Each year, at Thanksgiving, Nurse Jane puts up a good dinner for them, and I take the baskets around in my automobile."

"How nice!" gobbled the turkey. "May I help? I'm so thankful for not being in the oven, that I'd like to make some one else thankful too, if I could."

"That's the idea!" cried the bunny. "Yes, come along, Mr. Gobble Obble!"

Soon the bunny gentleman had filled his automobile with baskets of good things packed by Nurse Jane. Over the fields and through the woods rode Uncle Wiggily and the turkey gentleman, and many a poor animal family was the happier for Uncle Wiggily's visit.

And at last, when the final basket had been left, and Uncle Wiggily and the turkey were on their way back to the bungalow, out from behind a bush jumped the bad old Fuzzy Fox.

"I want to nibble Uncle Wiggily's ears for my Thanksgiving dinner!" howled the Fox. "I want ears to nibble!"

"Well, you can't—not to-day!" laughed Uncle Wiggily, and he made the auto go so fast that the Fox was left far, far behind.

"Oh, ho!" gobbled the turkey as they came within sight of the stump bungalow. "This ride will give us a good appetite for the Thanksgiving dinner."

"Indeed it will!" laughed the bunny.

But when they went inside, and met Nurse Jane, the muskrat lady looked at them in such a queer way that Uncle Wiggily asked:

"What is the matter, Miss Fuzz Wuzz?" (He sometimes called her that in fun.) "Has anything happened?"

"Yes, Uncle Wiggily, there has," sadly answered the musk-rat lady housekeeper. "I will not keep it from you!"

"Have—have they come after me?" asked the turkey in a faint and far-off voice. "Have they?"

"Oh, no," said Nurse Jane. "But by mistake I packed up everything in the house to eat in those Thanksgiving baskets, Uncle Wiggily! I didn't save out a thing for ourselves, and what to do about your Thanksgiving dinner I don't know! I'm so sorry——"

"Tut! Tut! Never mind," broke in Uncle Wiggily kindly. "I dare say we shall find something to nibble on. A couple of carrots will do me."

"Well, I have *those*," Nurse Jane said, "and a little corn."

"I love corn!" gobbled the turkey.

"I can eat it myself," the muskrat lady declared. "So if you can put up with that for Thanksgiving, we'll eat!"

Then they sat down to the corn and carrots, and Uncle Wiggily said:

"I'm thankful I could make the auto go so fast that we ran away from the fox."

"So am I," agreed the gobbler. "And I'm thankful I'm here sitting up to the dining table, instead of being nicely roasted on *top* of it! And I'm thankful I could help you feed the poor animal families."

"I'm thankful," spoke Nurse Jane, "because you two gentle-men didn't scold and make a fuss when you found what a mis-take I'd made about the dinner."

"Ha! Ha!" laughed Uncle Wiggily. "Then we are *all*

thankful, and there could not possibly be a better Thanksgiving than this!"

So they ate the corn and carrots and were very happy. And if the jumping jack doesn't waggle his tail like a skyrocket and knock over the milk bottles so they think they're roller skates and slide down the back stoop, I'll tell you next about Uncle Wiggily and the circus.

STORY XXIX

UNCLE WIGGILY AT THE CIRCUS

JACKIE Bow Wow, the little puppy dog boy, came running up to Uncle Wiggily one morning, so excited that he barked three times and fell down twice, stubbing his toe over a lollypop stick on the path.

"Oh, Uncle Wiggily!" barked Jackie. "What you think? There's pictures of elephants, and tigers and lions and camels! There's a man putting up a big tent! There are red wagons and golden chariots, and blue wagons and one that plays funny tunes!"

"And there's a man with his face all painted red, white and blue, just like your rheumatism crutch!" barked Peetie Bow Wow, the other little puppy dog chap, as he ran up wagging his tail. "And there's popcorn, peanuts and pink lemonade! Wuff! Wuff!"

"What's it all about?" asked the bunny rabbit gentleman, as he sat down on the steps of his hollow stump bungalow, while the puppy dog boys caught their breaths, which had nearly run away from them.

"It's a circus!" cried Jackie and Peetie just like twins, which they almost were. "A real circus!"

"A circus!" exclaimed Uncle Wiggily. "That's nice! Do you mean it is the kind you animal boys sometimes get up; where you charge two pins to get in and three pins for a seat?"

197

"Oh, no! It's a regular man-circus, that real boys and girls go to see!" barked Jackie.

"It's like the kind we once ran away and joined, where we learned to do jumping, to turn somersaults and other tricks," explained Peetie.

"Well, if it's that kind of a circus," spoke Uncle Wiggily, "we needn't bother our heads about it. We animal folk can't go to any real circus, you know!"

"Oh, but that's what we came to see you for!" whined Jackie. "We want you to take us to the circus!"

"Take you to the circus!" cried Uncle Wiggily. "Why, the very idea! How would an old rabbit gentleman and two funny puppy dog boys look walking into a real circus? The men would think we belonged to it, and had somehow gotten out of our cages. They'd shut us up behind the iron bars, as the lions and tigers are kept. Take you two to the circus! Oh, no! It couldn't be thought of!"

"Oh, dear!" sighed Jackie.

"We told the others that you'd take us," softly barked Peetie.

"What others?" Uncle Wiggily wanted to know, curious like.

"Oh, Sammie and Susie Littletail, Johnnie and Billie Bushytail, Lulu, Alice and Jimmie Wibblewobble, and a lot of the animal boys and girls," went on Peetie. "We were over on the edge of the woods, looking at the circus men put up the tent and the colored posters, and we all thought you'd take us."

"Baby Bunty will be so disappointed!" said Jackie.

Uncle Wiggily twinkled his pink nose serious like and thoughtful.

"Hum! Circus!" murmured the old rabbit gentleman. "So Baby Bunty wants to go, does she? Well, she never saw a circus, not even a make-believe one, such as you boys get up. Now I don't care for a circus *myself*—I've seen too many of 'em. But I'll go—just to take Baby Bunty!"

"And may we come?" asked Jackie, eagerly.

"Oh, well, yes, I s'pose so!" slowly answered Mr. Longears. "Nurse Jane will say I'm queer; but what matter? A circus comes but once a year! Now run along, doggie boys. I'll have to think up some way of getting all of you into the circus tent, for we can't buy tickets and go in the regular way. The circus men wouldn't understand."

Jackie and Peetie were so delighted that they turned somersaults all the way across the field as they ran to tell the other animal boys and girls. Meanwhile Uncle Wiggily hopped along on his red, white and blue twinkling nose——— Oh, listen to me, would you! I mean his rheumatism crutch. I guess I'm getting excited about the circus.

Anyhow Uncle Wiggily hopped across the field to the edge of the forest where Jackie and Peetie had said the big show was going to be given that afternoon. Surely enough there was the large white tent, much larger than the one the camping boys had used the time Uncle Wiggily helped dig a rain-water canal for the lads, so they would have dry beds to sleep in.

There was the circus tent!

And there were red, green, yellow, blue and purple posters showing pictures of lions, tigers, camels, elephants and all such wild animals.

"It's a regular circus surely enough," said Uncle Wiggily to

himself. "But how am I going to get in with the animal boys
and girls? I can't go up to the wagon and buy tickets, much as
I'd like to. I can't speak man-talk, though I can understand it.
How can I get in?"

Just then Uncle Wiggily saw two real boys slowly walking

"It's a circus, surely enough," said Uncle Wiggily.

around outside the big tent. They seemed to be looking for
something.

"I hope they haven't lost their ticket money," thought the
bunny. One boy said to the other:

"Here's a good place to get in!"

"All right! Crawl under!" exclaimed the other.

Then those two boys suddenly crawled under the circus tent,
because they had no money to buy tickets. Uncle Wiggily
watched them.

"Why! The idea!" exclaimed Mr. Longears. "What a way to get in! Why—I have it! That's how I can get in with the animal children! I can crawl under the tent! Of course I wouldn't do it that way if I could buy them tickets, and get in the regular way. But I can't—the ticket man wouldn't understand if I hopped up with green or yellow leaf money. Crawling under the tent is the only way."

Uncle Wiggily hopped back to the woods where he had built his hollow stump bungalow. The animal children were gathered about waiting for him.

"Come on. It's time to start!" said Susie Littletail, who had on her best hat made of green ferns.

"Where are you going, Wiggy?" asked Nurse Jane Fuzzy Wuzzy, as she saw the bunny gentleman starting off at the head of the procession of animal boys and girls.

"Oh, I'm just going to take Baby Bunty to the circus," said Mr. Longears, holding the littlest rabbit girl by her paw.

"Are you sure you aren't going for *yourself?*" asked Nurse Jane with a laugh.

"Of course not!" exclaimed the bunny. "The idea!"

On he hopped with the animal children, and when they came near to the edge of the woods, where the circus tent gleamed white amid the green trees, Uncle Wiggily said:

"Wait here, children, until I hop ahead and see if everything is all right."

The bunny, hiding behind a bush, looked across a little field at the tent. He saw two more boys walk softly up and try to crawl under the white canvas, but all at once a man with a big club rushed up, drove away the boys, and cried:

"No, you don't! You can't get in this circus that way!"

"Oh, dear!" thought Uncle Wiggily. "If men are on guard to keep boys from crawling under the tent, they won't let me in with the animal children! What can I do? Baby Bunty will be so disappointed! Ha! I know! I'll start here in this field, and dig a burrow, or tunnel under ground. I'll slant it down until I'm beneath the tent, and then I'll slant it up, so when we come out we'll be inside the tent. In that way the men with clubs will not see us!"

Uncle Wiggily hopped back to the waiting animal children.

"I'll have to dig a tunnel-burrow to get you into the circus," said the bunny. "Stay here and keep quiet!"

Starting in the field, behind the bushes and a little way from the circus tent, Uncle Wiggily began to dig. He was a fast worker, and soon he had dug the burrow all the way through.

He came out inside the circus tent, beneath the rows of seats on which were perched many boys, girls and grown folk watching the funny clowns, listening to the band, seeing the men on the high trapeze bars and looking at the horses.

"Ha! The circus is just beginning!" said Uncle Wiggily to himself, as the big bass drum boomed out: "Zoom! Zoom!"

He crawled back through the burrow and got the animal children in line.

"Forward march!" cried Uncle Wiggily, and through the underground burrow crawled the rabbits, squirrels, puppy dogs, pussy cats, chickens, ducks, guinea pigs and all the smaller animal friends of the rabbit gentleman.

They were not seen by the men with clubs, because they

crawled beneath the tent far below the ground. Then they came up inside the circus, under the high tier of seats.

"Oh, isn't it wonderful!" cried Baby Bunty, keeping hold of Uncle Wiggily's paw.

"Hush!" whispered the rabbit gentleman. "Don't let the people up above know we're down here or they might chase us out!"

So there sat Mr. Longears and his little friends, having a fine view of the circus almost from start to finish. And the people sitting on the seats above dropped peanuts and kernels of popcorn which the animal children picked up and ate. The only thing they didn't have was pink lemonade, but perhaps that was not good for them.

And at last, when the band began to play like anything, and the horses and elephants raced around the big ring, Uncle Wiggily said:

"Come, now. The circus is ended. We had better get out before the crowd starts or we may be stepped on. Did you like it, Baby Bunty?"

"Oh, it was the most wonderful thing I ever saw!" sighed the little rabbit girl. "Thank you, ever so much!"

"Yes, and we thank you also, Uncle Wiggily," called the other animal children.

Then they crawled down through the burrow again, outside the tent and came into the woods, through which they scampered to their different homes. But they had been to the circus!

And if the window curtain doesn't roll up so fast that it flies to the top of the ceiling, taking the gold fish with it, you shall next hear about Uncle Wiggily and the lion.

STORY XXX

UNCLE WIGGILY AND THE LION

ONCE upon a time, as Uncle Wiggily was hopping through the woods, he heard a roaring sound, coming, it seemed, from a distant clump of trees.

"Oh, ho!" exclaimed the bunny rabbit gentleman. "That's thunder! I suppose we are going to have a storm. I didn't bring my umbrella, but I can find a large toadstool, or mushroom. That will do as well."

The animal folk often use toadstools for umbrellas, you know, and Uncle Wiggily had done this more than once. The bunny hopped on a little farther, and the roaring, rumbling sound boomed out again.

"The thunder is coming nearer," thought Mr. Longears. "I had better hurry if I am going to pick a toadstool umbrella!"

He limped on his red, white and blue striped rheumatism crutch over toward a large mushroom (which, of course, isn't the same as a toadstool, though they look alike), and Uncle Wiggily was just breaking off the stem, so he would not get wet in the thunder shower, when, all of a sudden, a loud voice asked:

"Can you please tell me where the circus went to?"

Uncle Wiggily turned so quickly that he nearly lost the twinkle from the end of his pink nose. For the voice that spoke was almost as loud as thunder.

"Was that you making the noise like a storm?" asked the bunny as he saw a large yellow creature, with a great head, surrounded by a fluffy mane, and a tail on the end of which was a bunch of hair.

"It was," answered the big animal. "I'll try to speak more gently if it hurts your ears. But, naturally, I have a loud voice, being a lion, you know."

"Yes, I knew you were a lion. I remember seeing you in the circus," spoke the bunny gentleman, who was not at all afraid. "But tell me, why aren't you with the show now?"

"Because I ran away," the lion answered. "I got tired of being shut up in my cage all the while, and, when the man left the iron door open I slipped out. I've been hiding in the woods ever since; but it is not as much fun as I thought it would be. Now I wish I could go back to the circus. Can you please tell me where it is?"

"I am sorry to say I cannot," Uncle Wiggily answered. "But if you will come with me to my hollow stump bungalow—not that you can get inside, for you are too large—why, perhaps Nurse Jane may know where your circus is. She knows nearly everything."

"Who is Nurse Jane?" asked the lion.

"She is Miss Fuzzy Wuzzy, my muskrat lady housekeeper," replied the bunny gentleman.

"A rat, is she?" went on the lion. "I don't know much about rats, but once a mouse gnawed the ropes, when I was caught in a net, and set me free—that was before I joined the circus."

"Well, a muskrat is something like a big mouse," said Uncle Wiggily, "so I think you will like Nurse Jane."

"I'm sure I shall," the lion rumbled, trying to make his voice soft and gentle.

"Well, then," went on Uncle Wiggily, "please come along with me, and I'll try to find the circus for you. Nurse Jane may know where it moved to, or some of the animal boys and girls may tell us."

So Uncle Wiggily hopped through the woods, the lion stalking along beside him, and soon they reached the hollow stump bungalow of the bunny gentleman.

"Nurse Jane! Nurse Jane!" called Mr. Longears. "I have brought home a friend with me!"

"Not to dinner, I hope, Wiggy," remarked Miss Fuzzy Wuzzy, from inside the bungalow. "I have a dreadful headache! I haven't been able to wash the breakfast dishes yet, and as for making the beds, and dusting the furniture—it is out of the question! So if you want dinner——"

"Please tell her not to bother," whispered the lion. "I am not hungry and——"

"Is that thunder?" asked the muskrat lady, thrusting her head, tied up in a wet towel, from her bedroom window.

And when the muskrat lady saw the big lion she screamed.

"Pray do not be frightened, my dear Miss Fuzzy Wuzzy," the lion said. "I just came with Uncle Wiggily to inquire where I might find the circus, from which I foolishly ran away. But I'll toddle on, and not bother you, since you are ill."

"Oh, it isn't really any bother," spoke the muskrat lady. "I could get you a cup of tea. It was only your loud voice that startled me."

"I'm sorry," rumbled the lion, as gently as he could. "I'm

afraid my voice is rather louder than the purr of a pussy cat.
But I can't help it."

"Oh, of course not!" agreed Nurse Jane. "I wish I could ask
you in, but our bungalow was not made for lions."

"I'll come in and get him something he can eat outside,"
offered Uncle Wiggily. "By that time some of the animal boys

He ate nearly all
there was in
the
bungalow

or girls, who know where the circus went, may come along, since
you don't know, Nurse Jane."

"No, I am sorry to say I don't know," spoke the muskrat lady,
as she went back to bed with her headache.

Uncle Wiggily took some carrot soup and some lettuce tea
out to the lion, but though the tawny creature said he was not

hungry, he ate nearly all there was in the bungalow, for his appetite was much larger than that of the muskrat lady or Mr. Longears.

"And now I would like to do you and Nurse Jane a favor," went on the circus chap, licking the soup off his whiskers with his red tongue. "Couldn't I help wash the dishes or make the beds?"

"I'm afraid not!" laughed Uncle Wiggily, thinking how funny it would look to see a lion making a rabbit's bed.

"Yes, I suppose I am too large to get in the bungalow," went on the roaring chap, in as gentle a voice as he could make come from his throat. "But I know one way in which I can help!"

"How?" asked Uncle Wiggily.

"With my tail," said the lion. "That isn't too large to put through one of your windows. And on the end of my tail is a tuft of fluffy hair, just like a dusting brush. Please let me stick my tail in through the different windows. Then I can switch it around, and dust the furniture for Nurse Jane."

"Do you think you can?" asked the bunny, doubtful like.

"Of course!" said the lion. "True, I never before have dusted furniture in a bunny's hollow stump bungalow, but that is no reason for not trying. Please give me a chance!"

So Uncle Wiggily opened all the windows. The lion backed up, and thrust his tail first in one and then in another. When his tail was in the parlor he switched it around—I mean he switched his tail around—and the fluffy tuft of hair on the end knocked all the dust off the chairs, table and piano. Soon the parlor was as nicely dusted as Nurse Jane could have done it herself.

In this way, with his tail, the lion dusted all the rooms in the bungalow, even the one where Nurse Jane was lying down with a headache. And when the muskrat lady saw the lion's fluffy tail switching around on her chairs in such a funny way, she laughed, and then, in a little while, her headache was all better.

"You certainly are a good houseworker," said the muskrat lady as she got up and drank a cup of tea. "And you have done me a great favor."

"Pray do not mention it," spoke the lion politely as he flapped his tail in the air to rid it of dust. "It was a pleasure!"

Then along came Jacko Kinkytail, the monkey boy, and he said the circus had moved on to a town about ten miles away.

"Thank you! I'll travel there and get back in my cage," rumbled the lion. Then, with a polite bow to Nurse Jane and Mr. Longears, the tawny, yellow chap with the big voice walked away through the forest. And every time the muskrat lady thought of the lion thrusting his tail in through the window to dust the furniture she had to laugh.

Now would you like to hear a story abot Uncle Wiggily and the tiger? Well, you may if the scrubbing brush doesn't take the cake of soap out to the washrag's party and forget to bring it back for the bathtub to play ball with.

STORY XXXI

UNCLE WIGGILY AND THE TIGER

"UNCLE WIGGILY! Oh, Uncle Wiggily!" called a voice after the rabbit gentleman, as he was hopping away from his hollow stump bungalow one morning.

"What's the matter now?" inquired the bunny, turning around so quickly that his tall silk hat nearly slipped down over his pink, twinkling nose. "Does the Woozie Wolf or the Fuzzy Fox wish to nibble my ears?"

"I hope not!" exclaimed Nurse Jane, the muskrat lady housekeeper, for she it was who had called. "But will you please take my scissors with you, Uncle Wiggily?"

"Take your scissors? What for?" asked Dr. Longears.

"To have them sharpened," answered Miss Fuzzy Wuzzy. "They are so dull I can hardly cut anything, and I want to cut some linen up into new sheets and pillow cases. Take my scissors along with you, Wiggy dear, and have them made good and sharp."

"I will," promised the bunny rabbit gentleman. Then, wrapping the dull scissors in a grape-vine leaf, Uncle Wiggily put them in the top of his tall silk hat, and set the hat on his head.

"Why do you put them there?" asked Nurse Jane.

"So I'll remember them," the rabbit gentleman answered. "If I put them in my pocket I'd forget them. But now, if I meet Mrs. Twistytail, the pig lady, or Mrs. Wibblewobble, the

210

duck lady, and bow to them, I'll take off my hat.   Out will slide the scissors, and then I'll remember that I am to get them sharpened."

"That's a good idea," said Nurse Jane.   "Now don't forget to bring them back to me good and sharp.   If you don't I can't cut up into sheets and pillow cases the new linen I have bought."

"I'll not forget," promised the bunny gentleman.

He hopped on and on through the woods, and he had not gone very far before, all of a sudden, he heard a growling, rumbling-umbling noise, a little like far-off thunder.

"I wonder if that can be the lion again?" thought Uncle Wiggily.   "Perhaps he couldn't find the circus and he has come back to dust more furniture for Nurse Jane with the end of his tail stuck through a window in the bungalow."

Uncle Wiggily looked through the forest, but he saw no tawny lion.   Instead he saw, limping toward him, a beast almost as big as the lion, but with a beautiful black and yellow striped coat.

"Oh, ho! Mr. Tiger—the one I saw when I went to the circus with Baby Bunty!" exclaimed Uncle Wiggily.   "This is a tiger!"

"Yes, I am the striped tiger," answered the other animal. "And, oh, what trouble I am in!"

"What is the matter?" kindly asked the rabbit gentleman, for he could see that the tiger was limping and in pain.

"I ran a thorn in my foot," went on the black and yellow fellow, "and my eyes are so poor I can't see to pull it out."

"Perhaps I can," Uncle Wiggily said.   "I have strong glasses."

So the bunny gentleman looked through his spectacles, and soon saw the thorn that was in the tiger's foot. It did not take Uncle Wiggily long to pull it out.

"Oh, thank you, so much!" growled the tiger, though not in a cross voice. "It serves me right, I suppose, for having run away from the circus."

"Did you run away, too, as the lion did?" asked Uncle Wiggily.

"Yes," answered the striped beast, "we ran away together— the lion, some other animals and myself. But now I'd be glad to run back again."

"The lion was," said Uncle Wiggily. "He was very glad to go back."

"Don't tell me you have met *him!*" exclaimed the tiger. "Where is he?"

"He started back yesterday, after stopping at my bungalow and helping Nurse Jane dust the furniture with his tail through the windows," the bunny answered.

"Then I'm going back, too!" declared the tiger. "It isn't as much fun roaming by yourself through the woods as I thought it would be. I'm going back!"

"Before you start," kindly suggested Uncle Wiggily, "please come to my bungalow with me."

"Does more furniture need dusting?" asked the tiger, laughing. "I have no fluffy tuft on the end of my tail, as has the lion."

"It isn't that," the bunny answered. "But I would like to have Nurse Jane put some salve on the place where the thorn ran in your paw, and also wrap it up in a rag."

"That would be very nice," spoke the tiger. "Right gladly will I come with you."

So he limped through the forest with the bunny gentleman, and soon they came to the hollow stump bungalow.

"More company for you, Nurse Jane!" called the jolly rabbit uncle.

"That's nice," answered Miss Fuzzy Wuzzy. "Oh, you're a tiger, aren't you?" she went on, as she saw the striped beast.

"And he has a sore paw," spoke Uncle Wiggily. "Will you put salve on it for him, Nurse Jane?"

"Of course," answered the muskrat lady. And when the tiger's sore paw was nicely wrapped in a clean rag, he started off through the woods to find the circus.

"Good-bye, and come again," invited Uncle Wiggily, making a low and polite bow with his tall silk hat.

"I will," promised the tiger. And then the bunny suddenly exclaimed:

"Oh, your scissors, Nurse Jane! I forgot all about getting them sharpened," and he picked them up from where they had fallen when he took off his hat.

"Oh, dear! That's too bad!" said the muskrat lady. "And I wanted to cut the linen in strips to make sheets and pillow cases. Now it is so late I'm afraid the sharpening place will be closed."

"Perhaps I can help," said the tiger, turning back.

"Can you sharpen scissors?" asked Uncle Wiggily.

"No," was the answer, "but my claws are sharper than any scissors you ever saw. If you and Nurse Jane will hold the cloth, I will cut it into strips for you with my sharp claws. I don't need to use my sore paw. I'll take my other one."

"Oh, that will be very kind of you," said Nurse Jane. "I forgot that tigers have sharp claws."

So the muskrat lady and the rabbit gentleman held the linen cloth in front of the tiger, and with his claws he cut and slashed it into just the shapes Miss Fuzzy Wuzzy needed for making sheets and pillow cases.

"I am very glad I could do you this favor," the tiger said, when all the linen was cut.

"So am I," spoke Uncle Wiggily, "for if you hadn't been here to use your claws, Nurse Jane would not have forgiven me for not remembering to get the scissors sharpened. Good-bye!"

"Good-bye!" echoed the tiger, as he walked on to find the circus. And that night he slept in his cage again.

So if the doorknob doesn't try to crawl through the keyhole to play bean bag with the rice pudding in the gas stove oven, I'll tell you next about Uncle Wiggily and the elephant.

STORY XXXII

UNCLE WIGGILY AND THE ELEPHANT

"Matches, Uncle Wiggily! Matches!" cried Nurse Jane Fuzzy Wuzzy one morning, as the bunny rabbit gentleman was hopping down the forest path, away from his hollow stump bungalow.

"What's that? Patches?" exclaimed Mr. Longears. "Did I put on my garden trousers that have patches?" and he tried to twist his neck like a corkscrew, so he could look behind him.

"No, I didn't say 'patches'!" laughed Nurse Jane. "I said matches. Don't forget to bring me some matches to light the fire, when you come back from looking for an adventure."

"Oh! Matches!" repeated the bunny. "I'll get some for you, Nurse Jane."

Over the fields and through the woods hopped the bunny rabbit gentleman. He looked here, there and everywhere for an adventure, but could not seem to find one. The Woozie Wolf nor the Fuzzy Fox did not chase him to nibble his ears. Not that Uncle Wiggily wanted them to, but, if they had, that would have been an adventure.

"Well, perhaps I shall find one when I come back," said the bunny gentleman as he hopped along to the seven and eight cent store, where he bought a box of matches.

Carrying these fire-sticks in his paw, Uncle Wiggily was hopping through the forest, on his way back to the hollow stump

215

bungalow when, all at once, the bunny gentleman felt the ground trembling, and he heard a sound like a big horn being blown, and then a loud voice said:

"Oh, dear! I can't get it out!"

"Well, what can this be?" thought Uncle Wiggily. "That horn sounds like the big brass one I heard in the circus. From the way the earth shakes I'd say a big automobile truck was coming along. And as for someone who can't get something out—well, that sounds like trouble! I'd like to help, but first I must see who it is."

Uncle Wiggily looked through the bushes, and at first he thought he saw the side of some big house moving behind the trees. Then he noticed something like a great leaf flapping in the wind, and a moment later something long, like a fire hose, was thrust forward.

"Why, it's an elephant!" exclaimed the bunny, as he caught sight of the big chap.

"An elephant is just who I am," was the answer in a rumbling voice, coming through the rubber hose of a trunk. "I'm from the circus, and I wish I might be back there this minute, eating my hay!"

"Oh, so you have run away from the circus also, like the lion and tiger?" questioned the bunny.

"Yes," answered the elephant, "I did. But what do you know of my friends, the lion and tiger?"

"Oh, I have met them," answered Mr. Longears. "But is that your only sorrow—wishing you were back in the circus?"

"Indeed it is not," the elephant answered. "I have stepped on a loose stone, and it is fast between the toes of my left hind foot.   I can't get it loose by stamping on the ground, and I can't reach so far back with my trunk.   I'm in great pain and trouble!"

"That is too bad," spoke Uncle Wiggily.   "I guess your stamping on the ground is what I thought was an auto truck coming along."

"Perhaps," admitted the big circus elephant.   "I wish I could get that stone out from between my toes," he went on, stamping so hard that he shook the very trees, making them rustle as though a wind had blown them.

"Maybe I can help you," said Uncle Wiggily most kindly.   "I have with me my red, white and blue striped rheumatism crutch. With that I may be able to poke out the stone that hurts you."

"I wish you'd try," begged the elephant.

It did not take the bunny gentleman long to loosen the stone from between the elephant's toes, for the foot of an elephant is not like that of a horse or cow—he really has toes and toenails, just as you have, only a little larger, of course.   Well, I should say so!

"Ah, I feel much better, Uncle Wiggily!   Thank you!" spoke the elephant through his hollow rubber hose-like trunk, and it sounded like a trumpet or brass horn when he talked.   "Now that the stone is out of my foot I shall go back to the circus."

"The path to the place where the circus is now showing leads past my bungalow," said the rabbit gentleman.   "I'll hop along and point out for you the way.   I'd like you to meet Nurse Jane."

"That will give me pleasure, also," remarked the elephant, who was very polite.

So he and Uncle Wiggily went along together, but several times the bunny had to say:

"Please don't go so fast, Mr. Elephant. I can't keep up with you."

"I beg your pardon," spoke the immense chap. "Suppose I lift you upon my back and carry you that way?"

"I should much like that," the rabbit uncle said. So in his trunk the elephant gently lifted up Uncle Wiggily, and set him down on the broad back.

"Ah, this is even better than my auto," said Uncle Wiggily

"Ah, this is even better than my auto," laughed Uncle Wiggily, as the elephant crashed his way through the forest. Soon they came to the hollow stump bungalow.

"More company for you, Nurse Jane!" called Uncle Wiggily, with a laugh.

"Eh? What's that? Where are you? I don't see anybody but a big elephant!" cried the muskrat lady, looking up.

"I'm on his back!" answered the bunny. And as the elephant lifted Mr. Longears down in the trunk, Nurse Jane was so surprised that she hardly knew what to say.

"Will you—er—have a cup—I mean a *washtub* of tea?" the muskrat lady asked, well knowing that so big a creature must drink a lot of everything.

"Some water is all I need, thank you," answered the elephant. "I had something to eat in the forest before I met Uncle Wiggily."

Then the big chap put his trunk down in the brook and sucked up a great quantity of water. Uncle Wiggily put the box of matches down on the bench at the side of the bungalow, where the sun shone bright and hot, and watched the elephant drink.

"Well, now I'll travel along and go back to the circus," said the big chap with the large trunk and little tail. "I'll tell the lion and tiger I met you."

"Please do," begged the bunny, and then, all of a sudden Nurse Jane cried:

"Fire! Fire! Fire! Oh, the sun has set off the box of matches, and the bungalow is burning! Fire! Fire! Fire!"

Surely enough, this had happened. The box of matches, fizzing and spluttering, was burning Uncle Wiggily's bungalow.

"Turn in an alarm; Get the firemen! Call out the water bugs!" cried the bunny gentleman.

"Just a moment! Don't get excited!" spoke the elephant calmly. "I will put out that fire in a second!"

He sucked up more water from the brook in his trunk and squirted it on the blaze. The fire hissed and spluttered and died out in a puff of smoke.

"Oh, you have saved my bungalow!" cried Uncle Wiggily. "Thank you ever so much! Only for you I'd be burned out of house and home!"

"Pooh! That wasn't any more than you did for me—taking the stone out of my foot," said the elephant. "With my rubber hose-nose of a trunk, I very often put out little fires."

"Oh, I'm so glad Uncle Wiggily met you!" sighed Nurse Jane. "If he hadn't, our bungalow would have burned down, perhaps, Mr. Elephant!"

"Well, one good turn deserves another," laughed the elephant as he tramped away through the forest to find the circus, and the bunny gentleman and Nurse Jane waved "Good-bye" to the big chap.

So if the wheelbarrow doesn't catch cold when it runs after the train of cars to get a ride around the block, the next adventure will be about Uncle Wiggily and the camel.

STORY XXXIII

UNCLE WIGGILY AND THE CAMEL

"WHAT sort of an adventure do you think you will have to-day, Uncle Wiggily?" asked the muskrat lady housekeeper of the bunny rabbit as he hopped away from the hollow stump bungalow one morning.

"Well, Nurse Jane, I hardly know," was the answer. "I may meet with some of those queer circus animals again."

"I hope you do," Miss Fuzzy Wuzzy said, as she tied her whiskers in a bow knot, for she was going to dust the furniture that day. "The circus animals are very kind to you. And it is strange, for some of them are such savage jungle beasts."

"Yes," spoke the bunny gentleman, "I am glad to say the circus animals were kind and gentle. More so than the Pipsisewah or Skeezicks. But then, you see, the circus animals have been taught to be kind and good—that is, most of them."

"I hope you never meet the other sort—the kind that will want to nibble your ears!" exclaimed Nurse Jane as Uncle Wiggily put his tall silk hat on front-side before and started off with his red, white and blue striped rheumatism crutch under his paw.

"I hope nothing happens to him," sighed Nurse Jane as she went in to put the dishes to bed in the china closet.

But something was going to happen to Uncle Wiggily. You shall hear all about it.

221

On and on through the woods hopped the bunny rabbit gentleman, looking first on one side of the path and then on the other for an adventure. He was beginning to think he would never find one when, all of a sudden, he heard a rustling in the bushes, and a voice said:

"Oh, dear! I can't go a hop farther! I'm so tired, and my bundle is so heavy. I guess I'm getting old!"

"Ha! That sounds like trouble of the old-fashioned sort!" murmured Uncle Wiggily to himself. "I may be able to give some help, as long as it isn't the fox or wolf, and it doesn't sound like them."

The bunny gentleman peered through the trees and, sitting on a flat stump, he saw an old gentleman cat, looking quite sad and forlorn.

"Hello, Mr. Cat!" called Uncle Wiggily, cheerfully, as he hopped over toward the stump. "What's the trouble?"

"Oh, lots of trouble!" mewed the cat. "You see I'm a peddler. I go about from place to place selling pins and needles and things the lady animals need when they sew. Here is my pack," and he pointed to a large bundle on the ground near the stump.

"But what is the matter?" asked the bunny gentleman. "Don't the animal ladies buy your needles, pins and spools of thread? Just step around and see Nurse Jane Fuzzy Wuzzy, my muskrat lady housekeeper. She is always sewing and mending. She'll buy things from your pack."

"Oh, it isn't *selling* them that's the trouble," said Mr. Cat. "But I am getting so old and stiff that I can hardly carry the pack on my back any longer. I have to sit down and rest because my back aches so much.   Oh, how tired I am!   What a weary world this is!"

"Oh, don't say that!" laughed Uncle Wiggily, who felt quite cheerful that morning.   "See how the sun shines!"

"It only makes it so much hotter for me to carry the pack on my back," sighed the cat.

"Ha!   That is where I can help you!" exclaimed Mr. Long-ears.   "I am quite well and strong, except for a little rheumatism now and then.   That, however, doesn't bother me now, so I'll carry your peddler's pack for you."

"Will you?   That's very kind!" said the cat.   "Perhaps I may be able to do you a favor some day."

"Oh, that will be all right!" laughed the bunny, as he twinkled his pink nose.   "Come along, we'll travel together and perhaps find an adventure."

Uncle Wiggily slung the cat-peddler's pack up on his back, the pussy carried the bunny's crutch, and so off they started together through the woods.   They had not gone very far, and the bunny was wondering whether he could not sell Nurse Jane a lot of pins to help the poor cat when, all of a sudden, a loud, snarling sort of voice cried out:

"Oh, where can I find some water?   Oh, how much I need a drink!   I can go without one for seven days, but this is the eighth and if I don't see some water soon I don't know what will happen!"

"I wonder who that is?" asked the peddler cat.

"I don't know, but we'll soon find out," spoke Mr. Longears.

They looked through the bushes and there they saw a very strange animal, and not what you would call pretty, either.

This animal had a long neck, bent like the letter U, and his face looked as though he had rolled over on it in his sleep. But the queerest part of all was his back, on which were two humps, like little mountains, running up to peaks.

"Oh, what a queer chap!" mewed the peddler cat.

"Hush, don't let him hear you!" whispered Uncle Wiggily. "I think this is an animal from the circus."

"You are right—I am!" exclaimed the two-humped chap, looking toward the bushes behind which Uncle Wiggily and the cat were standing. "I heard what you said, too, Mr. Cat," the odd chap went on. "But I don't mind. I'm a camel, and I'm used to hearing folks say how queer I look. But I am in trouble now. Oh, dear!"

"What's the matter?" asked Uncle Wiggily, kindly.

"I'm so thirsty," the camel said. "You see, I took a long drink before I ran away from the circus, which I did, very foolishly, as I wanted some adventures. Well, I'm having them, all right! I've been lost in the woods, and, though I had enough to eat I couldn't find a thing to drink. On the desert, where I came from, I could find water once in a while. But here I'm lost.

"And, though I am a camel," went on the humped creature, "and can hold enough water in my stomach to last for several days, now my time is up. I haven't had a drink for over seven days, and unless I get one soon I don't know what will happen."

"Oh, I can take you to the duck pond and you can get a drink there, Mr. Camel," Uncle Wiggily said, as he hopped out from behind the bush.

"Oh, ho! What a funny chap you are!" snarled the camel,

not that he was cross, only a snarl was his regular way of speaking. "Are you a little camel?"

"Why, no, I'm not a camel," answered the bunny. "What made you think so?"

"Because of that hump on your back," said the camel. "Some of us camels have two humps, and some only one. But surely you cannot be a one-humped camel!   I never saw one with ears so long!"

"Indeed, I'm not a camel!" laughed Uncle Wiggily. "I'm a rabbit, and this pack that you see belongs to this poor peddler cat, who is too tired to carry it.   So I am carrying it for him."

"That is very kind of you," spoke the thirsty circus animal. "In fact, it seems to me you are very fond of being kind, Mr. Longears.   You carry the cat's pack, and now you offer to show me where to get a drink. And, if you can, I wish you would soon lead me to water.   I am very thirsty!"

"Follow me!" called Uncle Wiggily.   Then he hopped off through the woods, carrying the cat's peddler pack, and followed by the two humped camel, whose long neck swayed to and fro like a clock pendulum, while his humps shook like two bowls full of jelly.

Soon they came to the duck pond and there the camel put his queer face down into the water and drank as much as he pleased. He took a long time to drink, as camels always do, for they must take enough into their stomachs to last for a week in case they can not find more water before the end of seven days.

The cat and Uncle Wiggily stood watching the camel, thinking how queer and homely he was, but honest for all that, when, all of a sudden, out from behind a bush jumped the bad old Pipsisewah!

"Wow! Wow! I've got you now!" howled the Pipsisewah. "I'll nibble your ears now, Uncle Wiggily!"

The bunny rabbit gentleman started to run, but, because he had strapped to his back the pack of the cat peddler, the bunny could not hop fast at all.

"I'll get you! I'll get you!" cried the Pipsisewah.

"Oh dear! Oh dear!" sighed Uncle Wiggily, wondering who was going to save him, for he knew the tired old cat peddler couldn't.

And then, all of a sudden, the circus camel finished his long drink, and, with a jolly snarl, he cried:

"Here! You let Uncle Wiggily alone!" Then with his broad foot, made big and wide so it would not sink into the soft sand of the desert, the camel stepped on the tail of the Pipsisewah, holding him back so he couldn't chase Uncle Wiggily.

"Wow! Wow!" howled the Pip.

"Ha! Ha!" laughed the peddler cat. "Oh, mew!"

"Just wait until I get loose, and I'll chase you, too!" cried the Pipsisewah to the cat. "Just wait!"

"Don't be afraid!" said the camel, with a smile which made him look more homely than before, though this didn't matter. "Here, Uncle Wiggily, hop up on my back, between my two humps! You, too, Mr. Cat, jump up on my back. You and the bunny gentleman can sit there as the people of the desert used to ride me before I joined the circus. Hop up, my kind friends, and I'll soon carry you safe out of these woods. I can go fast, now that I have had a big drink of water. Hop up!"

Uncle Wiggily, with the cat's pack, hopped up on the back of the camel. The cat, too, sprang up. All the while the camel kept his broad foot on the tail of the Pipsisewah, so the bad animal couldn't get loose. And when the bunny and cat were safe in place, snuggled down in between the camel's humps, the queer creature started off, letting go the tail of the Pip.

"Ha! Now you can't get us!" mewed the cat, looking down from the camel's back.

"Just you wait! I'll get Uncle Wiggily yet, and you too!" the Pip howled. "And I'll fix you, Mr. Camel, for stepping on my tail!"

"Pooh! Nonsense!" snarled the camel, "Uncle Wiggily helped me by showing me where to find water, and now I am helping him." And away he went, quite fast, indeed, for such a queer chap.

And the old Pip skipped away to put some soft moss on his sore tail.

"Isn't this jolly!" laughed Uncle Wiggily, twinkling his pink nose. "I never expected to have a ride on the back of a camel! It's just like a circus parade! I wish Nurse Jane could see me!"

And the muskrat lady did, for the kind camel gave Uncle Wiggily a ride all the way home to the bunny's hollow stump bungalow, and when the muskrat lady housekeeper saw Mr. Longears up between the two humps she cried:

"My land sakes flopsy dub and a basket of soap bubbles! What will happen next?"

"I don't know," laughed Uncle Wiggily.

"As for me, I am going back to the circus," the camel said. And he did. The peddler cat, after selling Nurse Jane some sewing silk, stayed for some time with Mr. Longears, getting rested so he would be strong enough to carry his own pack of needles, pins and thread. And as for the bunny—well, he had more adventures, of course.

And the next one will be about Uncle Wiggily and the wild rabbit—that is if the teaspoon doesn't take the cork out of the bottle of bitter medicine and give it to the rag doll to make mud pies with.

STORY XXXIV

UNCLE WIGGILY AND THE WILD RABBIT

"THERE he is again!" cried Nurse Jane Fuzzy Wuzzy, as she ran to the window of the hollow stump bungalow and looked out. "He's digging up all the nice carrots in your garden, Uncle Wiggily!"

"Who is?" asked the bunny gentleman, laying aside the cabbage-leaf newspaper he was reading, with his glasses perched on his pink, twinkling nose. "Who is taking my carrots, Nurse Jane?"

"That wild rabbit," answered the muskrat lady housekeeper. "He lives in the thick bushes in the middle of the woods. I think he hasn't been here very long, and he doesn't seem to know any of your other animal friends. He's wild and runs the minute I go out. But he has been spoiling your garden lately."

"That isn't nice of him," said Uncle Wiggily. "I'll go out myself and see what he has to say."

But as soon as Uncle Wiggily started down the steps of his hollow stump bungalow, toward where the other bunny was digging up the carrots, the wild rabbit hopped away.

"What's the matter with you?" asked Uncle Wiggily, twinkling his pink nose in a friendly way. "Why are you spoiling my garden?"

229

"Because I like to!" answered the wild rabbit. "You live in a fine hollow stump bungalow, and all I have is a hole in the ground, or burrow. You're rich and I'm poor, and I'm going to spoil everything you have!"

"Oh, that isn't a good way to feel!" said Uncle Wiggily kindly. "That's the way the Bolshevics talk! I used to be poor, like you, but I went off to seek my fortune and I found it. I built me this hollow stump bungalow, and, if you like, I'll show you how to make one. Nurse Jane and I will help you!"

"Nope!" cried the wild rabbit. "I'd rather be bad! I'm going to dig in your garden every chance I get, and you can't catch me, either, so there!" And it sounded as if that wild rabbit might be making a funny "face" at Uncle Wiggily. Mind you, I'm not saying for sure, but maybe!

"Dear me!" thought Mr. Longears, as he went back in his house. "That wild rabbit is certainly a queer chap. I don't want to hurt him, but I wish he would get tame. I'll have to speak to Policeman Dog Percival about him, and set Percival on guard in my carrot patch."

"Did you make that wild rabbit stop his digging?" asked Nurse Jane, as she met Uncle Wiggily coming in.

"No, he says he's going to be bad," sighed the bunny gentleman, as he took his tall, silk hat down off the rubber plant.

"Where are you going?" asked Nurse Jane.

"Out in the woods to look for an adventure," answered Uncle Wiggily. "And perhaps I may find a way to make that wild rabbit tame and good."

"I hope so," sighed Nurse Jane. "It isn't nice to have our garden spoiled."

As Uncle Wiggily was hopping through the woods, over on that side of the forest nearest the village, where the real children lived, the bunny gentleman, all of a sudden, heard the voice of a little girl.

"Oh, Donald!" said the little girl, in sad tones. "You've broken it. You've spoiled my nice little jumping bunny!"

"Well, I didn't mean to," answered a boy's voice. "He jumped all right a minute ago!"

"Yes, but you went and squeezed the rubber ball too hard, that's what you did!" sobbed the little girl. "And now my nice Easter bunny won't hop any more! Boo hoo!"

"Dear, dear!" exclaimed Uncle Wiggily to himself. "This is too bad! There's trouble here! I wonder if I can help?"

You see Uncle Wiggily knew what the boy and girl were saying, though the bunny himself could not speak their talk. Uncle Wiggily hopped softly nearer the children. He looked through the bushes, and there he saw a little boy trying to mend a toy bunny for the little girl.

The toy bunny was made to look like a real one, with ears and fur and everything. Fastened to the toy was a little rubber hose and a rubber ball was on the end of the hose.

When the toy rabbit was placed on the ground, and the rubber ball was pressed, some air was squeezed inside the bunny's legs, and he would hop across the floor; and his ears would flop up, too, because he had springs and other things inside him.

"There's no use squeezing the ball," sadly said the little girl. "My toy bunny is broken, and won't ever hop again! Oh, dear! Boo hoo!"

"My! This is too bad!" said Uncle Wiggily. "I wonder

what I can do to make that little girl feel happier? I might get Sammie or Susie Littletail, the rabbit children, to come and stay with the real children for a while. They seem to be kind —this boy and girl. They wouldn't hurt Sammie or Susie. That's what I'll do! I'll go get the Littletail brother and sister, and have them hop over here so this boy and girl can easily catch them and play with them a while."

Uncle Wiggily started off through the woods. The boy and girl sat in a moss-covered dingly dell, trying to mend the broken toy. And Mr. Longears had not gone very far before, all of a sudden, he came to a little hollow place, filled with leaves. There he heard a voice saying:

"Oh dear! Oh what a pain! Oh what trouble I am in!"

"Ha! This seems to be my busy day for trouble!" exclaimed Uncle Wiggily, as he looked at the leaf-filled hollow. "Who are you, and what is the matter?" asked the bunny gentleman.

"Oh, I'm the wild rabbit," was the answer. "The wild rabbit who was eating the carrots in your garden. But alas! I can eat no more!"

"Why not?" Uncle Wiggily asked.

"Because I have fallen and broken my leg," was the answer. "I can hop no more, and I suppose I shall have to stay here and starve. I'm sorry I was bad, and tried to spoil your garden, Uncle Wiggily."

"Oh, perhaps you didn't really mean it," the bunny gentleman said. "But wait here a minute. I think I can help you."

"Oh, if you only would!" sighed the wild rabbit with a broken leg.

"I think I see a chance here," said Uncle Wiggily softly to

himself, "to help that boy and girl, and also the wild rabbit."

Off hopped Uncle Wiggily through the woods. It did not take him long to reach the place where the boy and girl had been playing with the hippity-hop rabbit toy that was now broken. The children were still there. The little girl had sat down on a log to cry, and the boy was trying to make her a willow whistle so she wouldn't feel so unhappy. The broken toy rabbit lay on a pile of leaves some distance away from the boy and girl. I suppose they had tossed it there, thinking it was of no more use.

"This is just what I want," said Uncle Wiggily. He found a long piece of wild grape vine, like a small rope, and, when the boy and girl weren't looking, Uncle Wiggily slipped up and fastened one end of the grape-vine cord to the broken toy. Then, hopping off behind the bushes, Uncle Wiggily began

"He's hopping off by himself!"

pulling the piece of vine. Of course he also pulled the toy rabbit along the ground.

"Oh, look!" suddenly cried the little girl. "Look, Donald! My toy rabbit is all right again! He's hopping off by himself!"

And, surely enough, the toy did seem to be hopping away. But this, as you know, was because Uncle Wiggily was pulling it by the grape-vine string.

"Come on! Help me catch him!" begged the little girl.

"I will!" her brother said. Together they raced on after the toy, which Uncle Wiggily jerked along the forest path. The bunny gentleman kept out of sight behind the bushes, and as the wild grape vine was just the color of the earth and leaves the children did not see it. To them it looked as if the toy was hopping away all by itself.

"I say, Mab!" called Donald. "He hops better than he ever did before! I wonder who is squeezing the rubber ball? I can't see anyone."

"Maybe it's fairies," suggested Mab, in a low voice.

"Pooh! There aren't any fairies!" laughed Donald.

On and on ran the boy and girl after the skipping toy rabbit, and Uncle Wiggily pulled it so fast as he hopped along, out of sight, that Donald and Mab could not get their hands on the toy. It kept ahead of them all the way.

Uncle Wiggily knew what he was doing and, in a little while, he led the boy and girl up to the place where the wild rabbit with a broken leg lay in the bed of leaves. Uncle Wiggily jerked the toy rabbit close to the wild one, and then pulled the toy out of sight behind a clump of ferns.

"Oh, Don! Look!" cried the girl. "Our toy rabbit has changed into a real one!" And she pointed to the wild rabbit, which could not move away, though he wanted to very much, as his heart beat very fast.

"A toy rabbit couldn't change into a real one!" said the boy.

"Well, mine did; else how could this live rabbit be here, and my toy one gone?" asked Mab. For that is what seemed to have happened, all on account of Uncle Wiggily.

"And see, Don," went on the little girl, as she knelt down beside the poor, wild bunny. "His leg is broken, just as my toy rabbit's leg was broken. Oh, it is the same one! My toy has changed into a live rabbit! Oh, you poor, sweet, lovely darling!" cried the little girl, as she cuddled the wild rabbit up in her arms.

"Say! This sure is queer!" exclaimed the boy. "Very queer!"

Uncle Wiggily, peering through the bushes where he was hiding with the broken toy rabbit, looked out and saw the little girl holding the wild rabbit with its broken leg. The wild rabbit would have hopped away if it could, but was not able.

"Oh, Uncle Wiggily! Uncle Wiggily! Is this how you help me?" sadly cried the wild rabbit. Of course, he spoke in rabbit talk, which neither the boy nor girl understood. But Uncle Wiggily, hiding in the bushes, heard and softly answered:

"Don't be afraid, wild rabbit. These children will be kind to you, I know. They will take you home, and mend your broken leg and you will be as stylish as I am."

"Oh, if I'm going to be *stylish*, that's different!" said the wild rabbit.   Then he nestled down in the girl's arms, and she and the boy took the bunny home and their father mended the broken leg with splints of wood and soft cloth bandages.

"Well, I guess that wild rabbit won't spoil my carrots any more," laughed Uncle Wiggily as he hopped along.   "I'll take this broken toy home to Sammie and Susie."

As for the wild rabbit, he was no longer frightened when he heard Uncle Wiggily say that the children would be kind.   And no one could have been more kind than were Donald and Mab. When the wild rabbit had to stay quiet until his leg healed, they brought him, every day, fresh lettuce and carrots, with cool water to drink.   And when the leg was all well, the wild rabbit was so tame that he never wanted to leave the boy and girl, and go back to spoil Uncle Wiggily's garden.   He lived happily with Donald and Mab all the rest of his life.

Sammie and Susie had fun playing with the broken toy, and they thought Mr. Longears was very clever to think of a way to not only help the wild bunny and the boy and girl, but also to save his carrots from being eaten.

So if the strawberry shortcake doesn't try to stretch itself up tall and look like a big mince pie, I'll tell you next about Uncle Wiggily and the tame squirrel.

STORY XXXV

UNCLE WIGGILY AND THE TAME SQUIRREL

ONCE upon a time, as Uncle Wiggily Longears, the bunny rabbit gentleman, was hopping through the woods, he heard a rustling in the bushes, and he crouched down to hide himself.

"For," thought the bunny, "this may be the Pipsisewah or the Skeezicks, or even the Woozie Wolf or the Fuzzy Fox. I had better be careful!"

But when Uncle Wiggily looked over the top of the bush, whence the rustling sound had come, all he saw was the tame rabbit, who once had a broken leg. The rabbit, who was now tame, was hopping along the forest path.

"Hello!" called Uncle Wiggily in his most jolly voice, as he twinkled his pink nose upside down, just for a change. "Where are you going, Tame Rabbit? I shall call you that as a new name. I hope you are not going to run away from Donald and Mab, the boy and girl who were so kind to you."

"Indeed I am not running away," answered the Tame Rabbit. "I am just going to the woods to look for some flowers. Don and Mab are going to have a little woodland party this afternoon, and I want to get them some flowers to put on the flat stump which they will use for a table."

"That is very kind of you," Uncle Wiggily said. "I'll help!"

"Wouldn't you like to come to the party?" asked the Tame

Rabbit, as he and the bunny gentleman hopped into the forest together. "There will be lots of good things to eat—even ice cream!"

"Thank you, I'd better not come, as some of the boys and girls might not be as thoughtful as Mab and Don," spoke Uncle Wiggily. "Some of them might throw peanut shells at my tall, silk hat; just for fun, you know."

"Well, perhaps they might," admitted the Tame Rabbit. "I don't wear anything but an old cap—nobody tries to knock that off," he added with a laugh. "But can't you just look in at the party, Uncle Wiggily? Just stop for a moment?"

"Yes, I'll do that," promised Mr. Longears. And when he had nibbled, with his teeth, some wild flowers for the Tame Bunny, Uncle Wiggily hopped to his hollow stump bungalow, promising to peek through the bushes at the children's party later in the day.

That afternoon, as he was hopping through the woods, Uncle Wiggily heard the sounds of shouting and laughter.

"That must be the party," thought the bunny gentleman. "I'll skip over and take a look."

In a little moss-covered dingly dell among the trees, Uncle Wiggily saw Don, Mab and many of their little boy and girl friends dancing about a broad, flat stump, which was set like a table. And in the middle was the bunch of flowers, some of which Uncle Wiggily had helped gather.

"Those children are certainly having a good time!" thought Uncle Wiggily, twinkling his pink nose so that it almost turned a somersault. "And the Tame Rabbit, who used to be wild, is enjoying himself, too." The other bunny surely was having fun, hopping here and there almost as if playing tag with the children.

All at once Mab cried:

"Come on now! We'll eat!"

"Hurray!" cried all the boys.

The girls didn't get so excited about it, but I think they were just as glad to eat as were the boys. The children gathered around the stump table, and I wish I could tell you all the good things they had for the woodland party. But I'm not allowed to do this for fear it would make you too hungry.

All I can say is that there was just the most lovely party-things you ever heard of! The Tame Rabbit sat near Don and Mab, eating what they gave him.

"Now we'll crack the nuts and play more games!" called Mab, after a while.

But when she went to pass the nuts she found that they were not cracked, and some of them had very hard shells.

"Oh, Don! Didn't you bring the nut cracker?" asked Mab.

"No, I thought you did," answered her brother.

"And I thought you did!" exclaimed Mab. "Oh, what shall we do?"

"We can crack the nuts with stones on top of the stump," said one boy.

But when they tried this, some of the nuts flew away over in the bushes, without getting cracked at all. Others hit the girls on the ends of their noses. And some of the children pounded their fingers instead of cracking the nuts.

"Oh, dear!" sighed Mab, as she saw what was going on. "My party will be spoiled, all because we haven't a nut cracker."

The Tame Rabbit heard all this. So did Uncle Wiggily, who was looking on, hidden in the bushes. Both bunnies knew what was said though they couldn't speak boy and girl talk.

"Can't you help the children, Uncle Wiggily?" asked the Tame Rabbit, as he hopped out to the bush where the bunny gentleman was hidden. None of the children saw the two animals talking together.

"How do you mean help them?" asked Mr. Longears.

"By getting them a nut cracker," went on the Tame Rabbit.

"A nut cracker?" exclaimed Uncle Wiggily. "A squirrel is the best nut cracker I know of. Ha! I have it! I'll send one of the Bushytail brothers over here to crack nuts for the children. I think the boys and girls will be kind to him. I'll go get Johnnie or Billie."

Away hopped Uncle Wiggily through the woods, and soon he met Johnnie Bushytail.

"Johnnie, don't you want to come and be a nut cracker for some children?" asked Uncle Wiggily.

"Why, of course!" chattered Johnnie, who was a very tame squirrel. "I love children," he said. "And I suppose I may eat a few of the nuts I crack."

"Oh, surely," answered Uncle Wiggily.

The bunny gentleman led Johnnie back through the woods to the children's party. The boys and girls were still trying to crack the hard nuts, but they could not do it well at all. Johnnie suddenly scrambled out of the bushes and up on the flat stump, and, taking a nut in his paws, he cracked it, by gnawing through the hard shell with his sharp teeth. Then he took out the meat and laid it on a birch-bark plate.

"Oh, look!" exclaimed Don, pointing to the Bushytail chap. "A tame squirrel is cracking the nuts for us! Look!"

"Maybe
he's a fairy!" she whispered.

"Oh, the dear little thing!" cried Mab. "And see, he's all dressed up like a real boy. Maybe he's a fairy!" she whispered as Johnnie cracked more nuts.

"Pooh! There aren't any fairies!" said Don. "But he sure is helping us!"

Johnnie sat up on the stump, his tail held straight up behind his back, and he cracked nut after nut.

"This is fine!" whispered the Tame Rabbit to Johnnie, the tame squirrel, while Uncle Wiggily, hiding behind a bush, saw and heard it all. "The children will love you for this."

"I'm glad of that," answered Johnnie, in animal talk, which

the boys and girls could not hear. Then the tame squirrel cracked many more nuts, eating some himself, for there were more than enough for all the children at the party.

"Oh, I wonder if we could take this squirrel home with us, as we took the Wild Tame Rabbit?" said the boy, as Johnnie cracked the last nut.

"Try it," suggested Mab to her brother.

But when Donald put out his hand, and tried to catch Johnnie, the squirrel boy just flipped his tail and scampered away.

"Thank you, I'd rather not be caught," chattered Johnnie, though of course Don and Mab did not know what he was saying. Then, when the woodland party was over, the children went home.

So that's how it all happened, as true as I'm telling you. And if the Jumping Jack doesn't stick beans in the sugar cookies, in place of the raisins he takes out to put in the molasses candy, I'll tell you next about Uncle Wiggily and the wolf.

STORY XXXVI

UNCLE WIGGILY AND THE WOLF

UNCLE WIGGILY was hopping through the woods with Nurse Jane one day, wondering what sort of an adventure he might have, and he was helping the muskrat lady housekeeper carry some clothes pins that she had bought at the three and four cent store when, all of a sudden, Miss Fuzzy Wuzzy called loudly:

"Look out!"

"What's the matter?" asked Uncle Wiggily. "Am I spilling the clothes pins?"

"No," answered the muskrat housekeeper of the hollow stump bungalow. "But, see that big wolf! Let's run!"

"Where's any wolf?" asked the bunny gentleman. "I don't see any," and he began searching in his pockets for his spectacles, which he had taken off, as they tickled his pink, twinkling nose.

"There's a big, gold wolf, over behind that mulberry bush," whispered Nurse Jane.

"What's that? A *gold* wolf? I never heard of such a thing!" exclaimed Uncle Wiggily. "You must be mistaken, Nurse Jane. I'll take a look!"

Then bravely singing the song—"Here we go 'round the

Mulberry Bush," Uncle Wiggily hopped up to where Nurse Jane pointed. Surely enough, something was gleaming gold-like among the trees, and as soon as Uncle Wiggily had put on his glasses, and had taken a good look, he cried:

"Well, well, Nurse Jane! This is a gold wolf, surely enough! But it cannot hurt us!"

"Why not?" asked the muskrat lady, who was getting ready to run.

"Because it is only a wolf carved out of *wood*, and painted like gold," answered the bunny gentleman. "I see what this is—it is one of the gilded wolves that were on the Little Red Riding Hood chariot from the circus. This golden, wooden wolf fell off the wagon and the circus people did not stop to pick it up."

"Well, I'm glad it's a wooden wolf," spoke the muskrat lady. "Then it can't nibble your ears; can it?"

"Not in the least," laughed Uncle Wiggily. "But if I had a wheelbarrow, or something, I'd take this wolf home to my bungalow."

"What for?" Nurse Jane wanted to know.

"Oh, I'd set it in the hall, near the umbrella rack," said Uncle Wiggily. "Just think! A golden, wooden wolf would be quite an ornament."

"Yes," agreed Nurse Jane, "it might look nice. But how can you get it home? It is too heavy to drag, and it has no wheels on as the animals have in the Noah's arks."

"Hum! Let me see, now," said Uncle Wiggily, walking around the golden, wooden wolf. "If I only had some wheels!"

And just then, along through the woods came Billie and

Nannie Wagtail, the goat boy and girl, each with roller skates dangling by a strap over their shoulders.

"Oh, Billie! The very chap I wanted!" laughed Uncle Wiggily. "Let me take your roller skates for the golden wolf! And you too, Nan!"

"With pleasure," bleated Billie, shaking his horns. "I'll help you fasten them on."

"Will the wolf bite?" asked Nannie, a bit timidly.

"Of course not!" laughed Uncle Wiggily.

So the roller skates were fastened on the paws of the golden, wooden wolf, and then, with a bit of wild grape vine for a rope, the gilded animal from the Red Riding Hood circus wagon was dragged through the woods to Uncle Wiggily's bungalow.

There the savage creature, who couldn't bite even a lollypop stick, was placed in the hall near the front door.

"Our friends will think us quite stylish like and proper," said Uncle Wiggily, admiring the wolf ornament.

"Yes," agreed Nurse Jane. "As long as it doesn't scare any of the animal children it will be all right."

But the animal children soon learned that the wolf was only made of gilded wood, and though his mouth was widely open, showing his sharp teeth, he could never, never bite them.

One day, about a week after he had brought the gilded wolf to his bungalow, Uncle Wiggily was home all alone. Nurse Jane had gone to the movies, with Mrs. Wibblewobble, the duck lady, and the bunny gentleman was just thinking of going to look for an adventure, or a piece of pie in the pantry, when, all of a sudden, there came a knock at his door.

"That must be Nurse Jane," said Uncle Wiggily. "She is

back a bit early, and has, I suppose, forgotten her key. I'll let her in."

The bunny gentleman opened his bungalow door, but, instead of his muskrat lady housekeeper he saw the bad old Skeezicks.

"Ah ha!" cried the Skeezicks. "I fooled you, didn't I? You thought I was Nurse Jane and you came to let me in! Now I'm going to nibble your ears! Ha! Ha!"

Uncle Wiggily tried to shut the door, but the bad Skeezicks pushed his way in, and was just going to nibble the bunny's ears when, all of a sudden, the impolite Skee saw the golden wolf.

Coming into the dark hall, as he did from the bright outdoors, the Skeezicks could not see that the wolf was not real. It looked so natural that the Skee stopped short and then he cried:

"Oh, excuse me! Oh, I didn't know you were here, Mr. Wolf, or I never would have come in. You are going to nibble Uncle Wiggily's ears, I suppose. You have the first turn. Well, I'll nibble them some other time, when you have finished. Please excuse and don't bite me! I'll skip right long!"

And with that, out of the door the Skeezicks jumped, never hurting the bunny gentleman at all.

"Ha! Ha!" laughed Uncle Wiggily, as he closed the door. "The golden, wooden wolf did me a good turn after all! He scared away the Skeezicks. I'm glad the circus wolf lives in my bungalow!"

And Nurse Jane said the same thing when she came home from the movies.

So this teaches us that it is a good thing to have something of gold around the house, even if it is only a gold dollar.

But now we have come to the end of this book. Not that Uncle Wiggily's adventures were over, for he had many more. But these are all I have room for here. Enough to say that the bunny rabbit lived happily for many, many years in his hollow stump bungalow in the woods, with Nurse Jane Fuzzy Wuzzy. And there you may, perhaps, see him some day.

Who knows?

ADIEU